THE FIRE ANT

Four men were murdered, a talented artist named Leslie Shippen, and three labourers named Holquin, Mendez, and Gomez. There did not appear to be any connection between the four of them, but that was what Inspector George Alvarado of the Los Angeles Police Department had to come up with, and he also had to come up with the identity of at least one killer — all in two weeks. He did it, but he also turned up a stunningly beautiful nude woman, and an elusive man known as Donald P. Robinson.

J. F. DREXLER

THE FIRE ANT

Complete and Unabridged

LINFORD
Leicester

First published in Great Britain in 1975 by
Robert Hale Limited
London

First Linford Edition
published 2004
by arrangement with
Robert Hale Limited
London

British Library CIP Data

Drexler, J. F., *1916 –*
    The fire ant.—Large print ed.—
Linford mystery library
1. Detective and mystery stories
2. Large type books
I. Title
823.9'14 [F]

ISBN 1–84395–423–0

Published by
F. A. Thorpe (Publishing)
Anstey, Leicestershire

Set by Words & Graphics Ltd.
Anstey, Leicestershire
Printed and bound in Great Britain by
T. J. International Ltd., Padstow, Cornwall

This book is printed on acid-free paper

1

Alvarado Versus Murphy

An individual fire ant was not actually much of a peril. If he crawled up a trouser-leg he could make a bitten person feel as though his leg were full of searingly hot little prickles of pain, but excluding the temporary discomfort, the surprisingly swift-acting venom of a fire ant's bite, no one died of the bite. Not of individual fire ant bites, but of course that was the entire point of the traditional fear of fire ants, they did not ordinarily come singly, and they had, perhaps not quite as often as it was alleged, killed human beings. They also killed large and small animals.

If they could swarm at night, which frequently happened, they could completely infiltrate a residence, killing everyone within it, right down to the pet cat and the dog.

They were known to have come upon sleeping kine, and to have swarmed over the beasts by the thousands, biting them, injecting their venom until death occurred to the beast weighing thousands upon thousands of pounds more than an entire itinerant swarm of fire ants.

As for *fearing* them, in Central America people feared what fire ants *could do*, but they had not much real reason actually to fear the swarms, not just because fire ants were predictable, but also because there were any number of simple precautions which could be taken to prevent the little nuisances from becoming dangerous.

At one time, though, in centuries past, fire ants had been literally dreaded by Central Americans in the countryside. There were innumerable legends of the incredible feats of those little creatures, mostly, in all probability, arising from the fertile imagination of the people who feared them.

The fire ant, then, passed into Latin American folklore, and legend as a menace who made people feel as though they had been set afire, when he bit them, and like the jaguar, *el tigre*, the anaconda, the hairy, great poisonous spiders, and the tiny, frail mosquito whose bite caused the *vomito*, yellow fever, the fire ant became a synonym for a variety of evil.

He came by stealth, oftentimes at night, and he attacked without provocation. The fact that he only killed in the collective sense, and not as an individual insect, did not change things. When someone was compared to a fire ant, it simply meant that he had the villainy of *collective* fire ants. It meant that he was stealthy, deadly, and probably unpredictably nocturnal.

But it could also mean that he travelled with a band of other villainous fire ants. Whatever it meant, someone so designated was not likely to be a desirable companion, and excepting someone whose vanity required this kind of an appellation, or someone whose ego throve on being classified as a menace, people generally did not cherish any such comparison.

In Latin America the connotation was not flattering. In other parts of the world, where fire ants did not exist, being called a fire ant meant little or nothing at all. But people did not necessarily have to know much about fire ants, or to have seen them or have heard the stories associated with them, to understand that when someone was termed a 'fire ant' he was not being flattered.

Detective George Alvarado of the Los Angeles Police Department had never seen a fire ant in his life. He had heard the Spanish term for fire ants, though, and he understood what it meant when used in connection with an individual, because, although George Alvarado's forefathers had not been South or Central Americans, had, in fact, been native Californians for hundreds of years, there existed an affinity among Spanish-speaking people, especially if they had a name like Alvarado, which allowed them to mix with all Spanish-speaking people, the assumption being that the affinity was strong, and so it was, up to a point, but it was also a little complicated, and a little different.

'You probably wouldn't understand it,'

George told Captain Murphy over lunch in Beverly Hills one pleasant spring day, 'and even if you did, it would seem pretty damned silly to you. But the gist of it is this: *Californian* Spanish is different from *Mexican* Spanish, as a dialect. *Californios* were never Mexicans, regardless of what people like you believe, Jerry, and *Californios* are the minority among U.S. minorities. But they are still considered sort of like cousins by all other pepper-bellies, even though strictly speaking, they are what the Mexicans call *Gachupines*, which is an insulting term, even though all it used to mean, in the early days, was someone who wore spurs.'

Captain Murphy held up a thick hand. 'That's enough. You're right, it sounds silly to me. A guy whose forefathers wore spurs is insulted when someone reminds him that *they* wore spurs. George, does that make any sense?'

Alvarado laughed. He was a grey-eyed, curly-headed, muscular man who looked to be in his thirties, but who could have been older. 'I told you, Jerry. I warned you. No, as a matter of fact, it doesn't

5

sound silly to me. But that's because I grew up understanding it. It *does* sound pretty damned anachronistic, though. Pretty damned old fashioned and long out of date.'

'Just tell me this: If your countrymen call this guy a fire ant . . .'

'Whoa. *Not* my countrymen, Jerry. My people were never in Latin America, not even in Mexico. They were growing beans, building cities, herding cattle, right here where this lousy restaurant sits, three hundred years before *your* people even knew there was such a place as California. Okay?'

Captain Murphy sipped coffee, examined the handsome man across from him with dead calm eyes, and said, 'Okay; you're touchy. I didn't know that. Okay; these people who are *not* your countrymen, then — why do they call this guy a fire ant?'

'Because in Latin America fire ants are stinging little insects that can kill people. They could have called him *el tigre*, meaning a jaguar, but my guess is that he isn't considered worthy of being classified

6

with that big cat, who happens to also be respected as well as feared. So — they call him the fire ant; the stealthy little bastard who sneaks up and stings you to death. Something like that.'

Gerald Murphy was a bull-necked, barrel-shaped, blue-eyed man with thin reddish hair and twenty-two years of police work behind him, most of it *not* in positions like the one he now held, Captain of Detectives, Westwood Division, Los Angeles Police Department and that meant that Jerry Murphy was not an aloof man. He did not know how to be aloof, even though captaincies in the LAPD were usually associated with aloofness, condescension, sometimes even haughtiness. For that reason he sipped his coffee and permitted Inspector George Alvarado to dress him down. Jerry Murphy was a 'results' man. He did not give a copper-coloured damn for honours, for a good press, for commendations from the Commissioner's office. He cared for results, good police work, and he believed those things were only achieved through hard work, long hours, minimal bellyaching, and teamwork. Maybe that was why Gerald Murphy had made it to a captaincy before retirement. It probably was.

He put aside the empty cup and returned to his sirloin steak. 'Would these people by any chance, know who the fire ant is? I mean, if they've named him, doesn't that imply something?'

Alvarado nodded. 'It implies that they consider him stealthy and deadly. That's all it implies. No, I don't think they know who he is.'

'But he's some kind of a — what should I say?'

Alvarado smiled softly. 'Pepper-belly. It's all right, despite what you think, I'm not touchy. This guy may be some kind of a Spanish-speaking national. All right, I'll accept that, except that it's only a possibility. Look; Spanish-speaking people in California — *Chicanos*, if you like that term — have been killed just like everyone else for a long time, and the killers have in fact been other *Chicanos*, now and then, but it's sure as hell no exclusive right, Jerry.'

Murphy threw up his hands. 'Just find him, George. Just get an identification, will you?'

'Why me?'

Captain Murphy lowered his arms and stared. 'What d'you mean — why you? You've just been bewildering me with a whole journal-full of stuff I never heard before, and which no other detective in our Division ever heard before, and then you ask — why me?'

Alvarado's quick grin returned. He ducked his head and resumed his meal. 'Okay. I'll put on my spurs and ride down Olvera Street and out through the *barrios*, the pepper-belly ghetto of Los Angeles. And you know what? The fire ant'll turn out to be some *gavacho*.'

'Some what?'

'Well, *you* call *them* pepper-bellies, beaners, and greasers. It's a two-way street, Jerry. *They* also have some endearing terms for *you*. *Gavacho* is one of them. It simply means . . . '

'Never mind what it means,' exclaimed Captain Murphy, hastily. 'I don't like being upset when I'm eating. It's bad for digestion. Just find this guy who has used the same routine to kill three local pepper — three local citizens of Mexican descent.'

Alvarado's grey eyes shone softly. 'You're all heart. You want three citizens avenged. Jerry, you're a law-and-order man. It doesn't matter to you that they were *Chicanos*.'

Murphy's broad brow curled. 'Is that sarcasm?'

'Maybe. Just a little.'

'Well, darn you, I'm not the only law-and-order man at this table. I've seen you go after murderers whose hides were as white as snow, and as black as the ace of spades. George, that's what it's all about, isn't it? I *am* concerned with law enforcement, and so are you. Right?'

'Right! By the way, is this lunch on your expense account, because if it isn't I'm in trouble. I've already reached my justifiable limit for the month. Last month, I got a nasty memo from your office saying . . . '

'All right! All right! It's on me.' Murphy beckoned for a waitress to re-fill their coffee cups, and after this had been done, he sighed with replete discomfort. 'I've got to move your vacation back a couple of weeks, George.' As soon as he had said this, Captain Murphy raised his hand. 'Now wait a minute, before you go sounding off. I've got four guys on sick leave this month, plus a full case-load, plus the fire ant.' He dropped his hand to the tabletop. We work together, don't we? We've got the best morale and the finest unit in the city, haven't we? And you're one of my best men. I rely on you, George, like I rely on damned few other people in the business — like I rely on damned few other people in this lousy world, if it comes down to that.'

For a moment George Alvarado gazed steadily across the table saying nothing, then he wagged his head. 'You Irish,' he exclaimed, 'are the biggest bull-slingers in the world.'

Murphy let that pass. 'It'll only take maybe a couple of weeks.'

Alvarado reached for his coffee cup. 'And you don't know *that*, either.'

Murphy's small eyes showed slyness.

11

'Of course I know it. You're one of the best in the business. It'll only take you a couple of weeks.'

Alvarado considered his companion with a candid, steady stare, then he said, 'Jerry, I knew, when you invited me to lunch, I was going to come out the short end of the funnel, some way or other.'

2

Alvarado's Intuition

The Coroner of the city of Los Angeles was a man of Japanese descent. In fact, he had been born in Japan. He had been a very controversial individual for years. He also happened to be one of the best men in the field of forensic endeavour in the entire country, which would have earned him national regard, if he hadn't also been a flamboyant, unnecessarily outspoken man.

Ordinarily, a coroner's department was the last place to find colourful people; the nature of the work did not customarily lend itself to the kind of extrovertism one usually associated with motion picture studios, but it was also a fact that if a department head was not restrained, his subordinates reflected some of this attitude.

When Inspector Alvarado went into the

City on a clear, benign springtime day to begin his investigation into the three murders allegedly perpetrated by someone Los Angeles' *Chicano* population called the 'fire ant', he anticipated the unusual, and he was not disappointed. The man he talked to, Charles Fisk, was young, at least five years younger than Alvarado, and met Alvarado, not as a city employee in the employ of the coroner's office, but as a fellow-investigator. He brought forth the files, expounded at some length upon the methodology of autopsies, and in the end, being slightly condescending, explained how it was that a knife, obviously in the same hand each time, had brought death to the three victims, all of Mexican descent, in a manner that was too consistent to have been handled by a different killer each time, something Alvarado had already worked out to his own satisfaction from police records. Then Charles Fisk blithely stepped out of the realm of his speciality, and invaded the speciality of Alvarado by saying, 'The affinity, here, is not altogether that these three men were local

Chicanos, but that all three of them were labourers, were roughly the same age, and lived in the same neighbourhood.'

Alvarado gazed at Charles Fisk without visible irony. 'Is that so?' he said quietly, and Fisk sensed the sarcasm.

His condescension faded slightly. He became a little defensive, and also a little antagonistic. 'It's our duty, in the coroner's office, to establish the means of death, and if we're convinced it was felonious, to explore the possibilities. The police have to rely on our findings, as you know.'

Alvarado agreed, with the same quiet irony. 'Yes, of course.' He then pointed to a page in one of the folders. 'This one — Mendez — was a narcotics addict.'

Fisk leaned to look downward. 'Yes.'

'But the other two were not.'

Fisk shrugged. 'If it says so. Our files are completely reliable.'

'One of the others — Holquin — had an old bullet wound.'

Fisk nodded. 'I remember Holquin. I assisted in the posting. In fact, I did the research on that old scar. He was a

15

purple-heart veteran from Korea.'

Alvarado nodded. 'But neither of the other two were ever in the army.'

Fisk paused. 'What are you getting at, Inspector?'

'That there doesn't really seem to be much of an affinity among them, as individuals. As for living in the same neighbourhood, *Chicanos*, like everyone else, tend to live among their own kind.'

'They were all labourers, Inspector.'

'Yeah. So I noticed. So are thousands of other men, who aren't *Chicanos*.'

Fisk gazed steadily at the slightly older man. 'Are you implying something?' he asked coldly, and Alvarado gave his disarming, ready smile, before answering.

'Only that I don't know much about autopsies, Charles, and you don't know much about murder investigations.' He closed the last file and left it lying upon the desk as he glanced at the wall-clock. 'There *is* an affinity, but it's not that those three guys lived in the same part of town, or ate *tortillas*.'

'Is that so?' stated Charles Fisk, showing hostility in the face of George

Alvarado's smile. 'And what is it?'

'That Mendez, Holquin, and Gomez were not members of the labourers union.'

Fisk continued stonily to regard Inspector Alvarado for a moment, then he loosened his stance, and sighed. 'I see. And you think this had something to do with it.'

Alvarado continued to smile. 'No. Let me tell you something, Charley: The surest way that I know to end up 'way out in left-field during a murder investigation, is to pick out seeming relevancies, and try to bend them to fit an idea. Pick them out, if you like, and remember them, but that's all; don't try to read a significance into them, until there is some kind of hard evidence to support them — and even then, don't try to *make* facts, let the facts develop.' Alvarado glanced at the clock again. 'You've been a big help. Thanks a lot.'

He left Fisk's office, left the big stone pile where the coroner's establishment resided, and walked thoughtfully back to his car. He had done considerable homework since the previous day when he'd had luncheon with Captain Murphy, had read transcripts, had gone over each report of the initiating officers, and had rather exhaustively researched the background of the murder victims, Mendez, Holquin, and Gomez. Finally, he had seen the coroner's files.

He would have been justified in seeking out the survivors of the victims, but the first officers on the scene at each separate murder had filed professional reports. There were probably a few things still to be gleaned, because such a condition always existed; no one remembered *everything*, especially while the shock was still fresh, but that could wait.

Alvarado needed an affinity, exactly as the coroner's man had implied. It would be impossible to make sense out of those three killings until the affinity was located, but the killer dubbed the 'fire ant' by an aroused Mexican-American community, whose designation had been adopted by the press, was not through, Alvarado was convinced of that, and this was currently his prime concern. He wanted, first of all, to prevent additional murders. Secondly, he wanted to discover what someone who was very expert with a knife, had in common with three men who had not known one another, had never worked on the same jobs together, and, except for a common Latin heritage, actually had practically nothing in common.

The murderer could of course have been a madman. Alvarado hoped not because unpremeditated murder was almost impossible to resolve, unless the murderer helped a little.

A man who, while strolling a crowded daytime sidewalk in the heart of the city's shopping district, and who perhaps suddenly was told by 'God' to stab the person walking directly ahead of him, was the hardest of all killers to apprehend, and — it had happened any number of times — even if he *was* apprehended, he frequently looked at the accusing police-man with a perfectly blank face, and had no recollection at all of having murdered anyone.

One of the local newspapers had come

up with this possibility. A detective George Alvarado had worked with on other cases, had brought him a copy of that newspaper with a sardonic comment.

'For your sake, George, I hope they're wrong. If he's a nut, you're only going to find him when he misses with one of those slashes someday, and some guy kicks him to death, or some cop shoots him.'

Alvarado had smiled. 'Let it be tomorrow.'

He did not even have a description. One of the unique things about murders in the city, where thousands of people could be expected to be within shouting distance of every crime which was committed, there were rarely ever any witnesses.

He did not even believe that this was strictly some kind of *Chicano* affair, despite the fact that the three dead men had all been of Mexican, or Latin American, descent. The reason he did not believe this, was because he and a dozen other detectives with names like Alvarado, Camacho, Lopez, and so forth, all of them with good contacts and sources of information down in Mex-town, and who cooperated closely together, had not received a single hint of ethnic trouble in the city.

But he would not have made this argument to Captain Murphy, or most of the other detectives in the Department, who invariably viewed more than one slaying in Mex-town in the same week, as the result of some secret, dark and ominous dissention among the *Chicanos*, the people of Latin American descent, whether Mexican, Puerto Rican, Cuban, Bolivian, or whatever.

He had friends in the *Chicano* organisations such as the *Falcones*, a strongly conservative, racially-oriented semi-militant organisation whose expressed purpose was to protect the civil rights of its members — who had to be of Latin American origin, or descent, to belong. He talked to a man named Mike Zapata for almost a full hour after returning from the coroner's office, and came up with what he already suspected: There were no ethnic rumbles in the making in the *barrios*, the *Chicano* neighbourhoods. There had been, Zapata said, a little trouble with some pushy blacks a couple of months back, but it had died aborning, and there had been rumours of Cuban revolutionaries infiltrating, with a view towards starting civil violence, but that, too, hadn't got off the ground.

The reason, according to Miguel Zapata, it hadn't amounted to anything, had a lot less to do with the usual sympathy *Chicanos* manifested towards Latin Americans who were dedicated to opposing the U.S. Establishment, than to something one grizzled, greying Cuban expatriate had said at a rally.

'Sure as hell we're oppressed. We work five days a week, we eat meat seven days a week, we make a couple of hundred dollars a week, and me — personally — I drive a new Ford to meetings like this, where I cry great tears like all the rest of you, over being so damned oppressed. Let me tell you, *barbudo*: When guys like Fidel Castro get things down there so good they can hire me for two hundred dollars a week, let me know, will you?'

According to Mike Zapata the shouting, laughter, and feet-stamping which had followed this man's statement, had broken up the meeting. Zapata had then told Alvarado he would, personally, make enquiries, and if he turned up anything at all he thought might help the police investigation, he would call back.

Alvarado did not expect to hear from Mike Zapata, and he didn't hear from him.

He also talked to an editor of the largest Spanish-language newspaper in Los Angeles, a man named Morales. All Morales had told him was: 'Wait; wait until there's a recession, *then* ask me if there's trouble coming. Right now, the best you're going to come up with, George, is something personal. These three guys were sleeping around, something like that, and got caught.'

Alvarado had put down his telephone after that call, with a shake of the head; *three* men were not sleeping around, and had got caught and were knifed to death in the exact same manner, because all three men would have had to have been sleeping around with the same woman, whose husband killed them all in the identical manner. That was asking an awful lot of one man's wife.

The ethnic thing was out, obviously, which left George Alvarado just about where he'd been the day he and Captain Murphy had had lunch. He went home that evening pondering his options, and decided that he had to request two things: One, a diligently undertaken delving by his informants among the *Chicanos*, and a search among the backlog files at the coroner's office, among the cases involving knife slayings.

Otherwise, he had to put out inter-departmental feelers for information on recent knifings, which had *not* been fatal, then, finally, he had to undertake a file-search through channels in an effort to locate someone whose *modus operandi* fit the kind of knifings which had ended three lives. And he had to come up with something, from at least one of these sources, perhaps all three of them combined, which would permit him to resolve his assignment within two weeks.

Captain Murphy had said he could do it in two weeks. Captain Murphy had also been indulging in some of his expert buttering up, but even though they had both known Alvarado had understood exactly what Captain Murphy had been doing, nonetheless the bare facts were that Captain Murphy *did* rely very heavily on Alvarado, and that, too, was something Alvarado knew. For this reason, then, he would do precisely what Captain Murphy had expressed satisfaction about, he would do his utmost to resolve the fire-ant killings within two weeks.

And he laughed at himself for being manipulated like this, when he knew that was what was happening.

3

Leslie Shippen

A great Latin American liberator had once said of a friend that he had done more than enough to deserve success. It was the kind of rhetoric Latins loved to hear, or to read, and as George Alvarado told Captain Murphy the fourth day of his investigation into the fire-ant affair, it did not mean a lousy damned thing, it was just a handful of nice-sounding words strung together, which appealed to people who were by nature gullible enough to think a vastly profound observation had been dropped upon them.

George's irritability was prompted by Captain Murphy's visit to Alvarado's office, where George was ploughing through the results of his inter-departmental search hoping to find a recent knifing which had not produced a fatality, where the pattern had been similar to three knifings which *had* produced fatalities. Murphy, seeing the pile of papers, had made some remark about like the one made long ago by the Latin American liberator, and that had sparked George's annoyed outburst.

Then Captain Murphy had handed across a yellow piece of paper from the tele-printer down in Communications, without saying a word. Afterwards, while George read the message, Captain Murphy had gone to a chair and got comfortable, await-ing the eruption he was certain to come, and which in fact did come, when Alva-rado put down the yellow piece of paper, glanced momentarily at the untidy mass of work atop his desk, then said, 'You see; it's ridiculous to say someone deserves success, isn't it? There is another knife victim, right while I'm trying to figure out a way to prevent something like that.'

Murphy was calm. 'How could you prevent something you don't know anything about?'

Alvarado leaned to re-read the yellow piece of paper. 'Fisk. That's the guy from the coroner's office who can divine the future from looking at peoples' insides.

Or something like that.'

Murphy was unimpressed. 'Is he qualified to say this one is exactly like the other three?'

George nodded his head. 'He's qualified. He's also a pain in the tail.' George continued to study the yellow paper. 'Okay; I deserved success, but I didn't get it. So much for that. So much for all this inter-departmental rubbish on my desk. I wasn't very hopeful about coming up with the identity of the fire ant from this stuff, anyway.'

Captain Murphy said, 'This time the victim is a *gavacho*.'

Alvarado's grey eyes shot upwards. 'You remembered.'

'No; I just met Eric Lopez in the corridor and asked him what it was *they* called *us*. He told me.' Captain Murphy smiled, having bombed out on his *mot*. 'Not only was this victim a *gavacho*, he also happened to be a comfortably well-off professional artist and illustrator. If there's a connection between him and those three *Chicano* victims, it ought to be very interesting.'

Alvarado nodded absently, stared a moment at the telephone, then plucked it from its cradle and dialled the coroner's office. He did not particularly want to speak to Charles Fisk, but there was no choice, so, when Fisk came on the line, saying his name crisply, Alvarado identified himself, then said, 'Charley, until I've talked to the initiating officers, I'd like your opinion: Could this latest victim have been done in by someone who read in the newspaper how those other three men were killed?'

Fisk's answer was candid. 'I suppose so, but the probability of someone simulating that identical thrust so perfectly, would seem to me to be rather unlikely, Inspector. And there is this other thing.'

'What other thing, Charley?'

'We have perfected a forensic technique in this office which is certainly unique enough to deserve world-wide recognition, Inspector. We have just finished freezing the lacerated parts of Leslie Shippen, the latest victim, which allows us to make both microscopic and photographic comparisons with the similarly lacerated organs of the other three victims — and will shortly now inform your office by letter that the knife used in each of the four cases was the same weapon. It has two very small chips in the blade. They only show up when the lacerated organs have been frozen.'

George was honestly impressed. He rang off, told Captain Murphy what Fisk had said, then he arose to leave, and Captain Murphy, also arising, said, 'Good luck.'

On his way out of the building Alvarado put in a request for whatever was on file with LAPD concerning a man named Leslie Shippen. He also requested a check-out with the FBI, not because he expected anything from this source, but because such a request was routine in capital crimes. Finally, he checked with the Duty Officer of the uniformed division to ascertain when the patrolmen who had first arrived at the scene of the Shippen murder would be checking in, then he went forth into the sunshine to drive off in the direction of the address of the murder victim, as given on the yellow teleprinter report.

Perhaps the most recent killing performed by the fire ant bore his particular stamp, but this time the crime had been committed in an altogether different part of the city. There was not much similarity between Palm Drive in Beverly Hills, and the *Chicano* district which was sandwiched between two heavy industrial areas in an altogether different part of the city.

The body had been taken away, there was still a team of laboratory men at the skylighted, very elegant and expensive apartment of Leslie Shippen, when Inspector Alvarado arrived, and there were also two other homicide detectives on hand. Neither of them were men Alvarado knew except very casually, and his arrival did not seem to impress the pair of men in the slightest. He did not need anything from them. There was a chalked outline where the body had been lying. The apartment was very neat, there was no sign of any kind of a struggle, any variety of disturbance of any kind, and where the sun streamed through upon an artist's easel which had a cloth over the canvas upon the easel, several black-handled brushes stood in a strong-smelling mixture of some kind, probably a solvent.

In fact the entire front of the apartment, which had been Leslie Shippen's studio, smelled strongly of solvent, but in the bedroom, which opened off the studio, the small kitchenette, dining alcove, bathroom and dressing room, the solvent-scent was not detectable at all. Evidently Leslie Shippen had made a point of keeping the intervening door closed.

One of the beefy detectives who had been conducting an initial investigation, left the room to use a telephone on the wall in the kitchenette. The other one strolled over partially to block the streaming sunshine coming through the high, narrow, leaded-glass window, and jabbed a thick thumb at the covered canvas.

'Take a look at that,' he said to George Alvarado. 'This guy was a good artist.'

Alvarado lifted the damp cloth. As he stood looking at the painting, the beefy man chuckled. 'See what I mean?' he said to George. 'We were wondering — did this guy paint that nude girl from memory, from imagination, or from a pose?'

Alvarado did not comment. The painting was almost alive. As the beefy man had said, Shippen was a good artist. The girl was beautiful. Even with her clothes on, she would have caught Alvarado's eye, any time, any place. Without her clothes, she was strong and muscular without lumps. She was golden, with tawny large eyes and coppery hair. She was standing against a sea-green background looking slightly to her left, as though caught in an attitude of mild surprise.

Alvarado continued to look as he said, 'What's her name?'

The detective shrugged massive shoulders. 'That's where my partner went, to see who's been coming up here lately. If she was a model, then maybe we've got something.' With his view of the magnificent nude woman cut off, the beefy older man reverted. In a calm, hard-sounding tone he said, 'The guy had fifteen hundred dollars in cash in his pants-pocket. He had a diamond ring on his left hand big enough to choke a horse. It doesn't look like robbery, but you can't ever be certain, can you?'

The other detective returned. 'No luck,' he announced as he passed into the apartment. 'The landlord's not home, and the only tenant I could scare up is some guy who works nights and sleeps like a log during the day. He didn't see anything or hear anything.' This detective looked a moment at Alvarado as he crossed the studio. Then he said, 'I also called in. It's your baby, Alvarado. We're to go out on a forgery case.'

After the two beefy men had departed, Alvarado lifted the cover over the last painting to be completed by Leslie Shippen, raised a finger to test the moistness upon the canvas, then gently lowered the cover and turned very slowly making a thoughtful survey of the studio.

Where the corpse had been outlined, was distant from a chair or a sofa about eight or ten feet, and while it was impossible accurately to predict the position Leslie Shippen had been facing when he'd been knifed, Alvarado thought he had probably been facing the door, which was another eight or ten feet distant.

A reasonable assumption was that Shippen had just admitted someone to his studio, had perhaps taken three or four steps back towards the centre of the room, and possibly in response to something his visitor had said, or had done, faced about, back in the direction of the door, or at least the front wall. He had then been knifed. Whether he had fallen back and had not moved afterwards or not, did not seem entirely relevant at this stage, but Alvarado doubted that he had not moved after falling; a deep knife thrust, even when done as expertly as the fire ant managed his thrusts, did not have the same shock-power a bullet had. Instantaneous deaths from knife thrusts, unless they went directly into the heart from one side or the other of the sternum, were not at all common.

One thing was reasonable to assume: Leslie Shippen had probably known his assailant, and that might prove helpful. On the other hand, a professional illustrator might have opened the door to someone he'd never seen before, professing to be a potential customer. The reason Alvarado was inclined towards the belief that Shippen and his killer were not strangers, was a groundless assumption that the statuesque woman in the fresh painting had been a live model, in the room at the time Leslie Shippen had admitted his killer. It did not seem probable to Alvarado that Shippen would have subjected the beautiful, naked girl to ogling by some un-announced caller.

This was pure conjecture, but he had a minor reason for liking it. The solvent-less scent of the inner apartment had a faintly discernible fragrance of an expensive perfume. Leslie Shippen had undoubtedly turned over his bedroom to the model to undress, and later, to re-dress.

So — there had been a witness. Not necessarily a witness to murder, but very likely a witness to the arrival of the caller.

Well; *possibly* there had been a witness.

He turned to the painting, studied it again, then went to a beautiful, carved rosewood desk and rummaged for whatever it had to offer in the way of a list of models, or modelling agencies.

He found not one list, but four. He also found a nickel-plated .32 automatic pistol with mother-of-pearl handles, a full clip, and a loaded chamber under the hammer. In a lower drawer he found something else he would not normally have associated with an artist, or an artist's studio, although as he was to figure out later, artists used all manner of life-like objects in their work. He found two daggers, one evidently very old, heavily engraved and inlaid with gold and silver, the other dagger painfully plain in contrast, and entirely functional without any kind of ornamentation, unless the handle, which had been made of some variety of thick, heavy bone, could be classified as ornamental.

He appropriated the models' lists, left the pistol and daggers where he found them, and went on through into the private apartment beyond to complete his rummaging.

The telephone rang as he was leaving the studio, but by the time he could get out where it was, in the immaculate little kitchenette, it stopped ringing. He thoughtfully regarded it, on the wall, wondering why anyone who would bother to telephone someone, would only allow the telephone to ring three times.

Then he turned to the work of painstakingly going through the effects of the late Leslie Shippen, and with all afternoon before him, and without the slightest fear of being caught doing this by the owner of the personal effects he examined, Alvarado took his time.

4

A Warming Trail

He left the serial number of the pearl-handled automatic pistol in Ballistics for a possible identification, went along to speak to the uniformed officers who were first on the scene, and in their wardroom while they were getting out of harness, picked up the first encouraging information of the day. One of them said there was a definite scent of perfume in Shippen's private quarters off the studio, when the uniformed men had first arrived, and without anything to base it upon, they had decided between themselves that the beautiful woman with coppery hair who was driving away in a robin's-egg-blue MG with red leather upholstery, when the police cruiser first arrived, might have been the female who had been in Shippen's bedroom. The reason they thought this was possible, was that her perfume was still very faintly discernible in the entrance to the building when the officers had walked in. And there was another matter. According to the dispatcher who had sent the patrol car to the elegant, Spanish-type apartment building, it had been a woman with a strong, youngish voice, who had called in, for the police. All she had said was that the police were needed at once, and gave an address but according to the uniformed men, it all fit fairly well, even though it was without one damned bit of conclusive evidence, and George Alvarado was inclined to agree.

When he got back to his office, a technician named Andrews with whom he had worked before, telephoned to say they had an identification on the pearl-handled pistol. It had been sold new to one Leslie Shippen, an illustrator, and Andrews gave Shippen's address. In the place on gun-permit forms where it was asked why an applicant wanted to own a concealable weapon, Shippen had written 'self-protection'. But, as Alvarado knew very well, nine out of ten applicants said this; were in fact told by the police to say it, because it was the best reason a man could give, and was just about the only reason which was acceptable to the granting authorities.

So much for the gun. Alvarado thanked Andrews, rang off, spread the list of models and model agencies before him atop the desk, and was leaning to begin his study of them, when Files and Records called to report the results of their ID file search on Leslie Shippen. They had run the name through the Los Angeles FBI offices, but the federal agency had nothing which LAPD did not already have, and none of it was very startling. Shippen had once been arrested for possession of narcotics paraphernalia, but without narcotics in his possession, too, and because his alibi proved out — he had been preparing a series of illustrations requiring narcotics-users equipment — he had been released.

Otherwise, aside from several traffic citations, which automatically went into everyone's record, as a matter of routine, Leslie Shippen had only one other record of arrest in his file. He had been involved in a race-track swindle in which another man, a friend of Shippen's, had perfected a smooth way for the race-track to be defrauded of almost one million dollars. It had been a rather simple scheme. Shippen's friend had simply duplicated, through a series of forged printings, all the betting tickets offered as receipts to betters, for one race. And while this had taken a bit of doing, when the race had been run, Shippen and two other men had presented their forged winners' tickets, and had been paid off. They were still making their rounds of the pay-off windows when alert plainclothes, private race-track police, had noticed the same men consistently collecting, and stuffing vast amounts of money into valises they carried. The possibility of this kind of surveillance being in force at the race-track had been quite overlooked. Perhaps it had not even been known that race-tracks did in fact have excellent security establishments.

In any case, Leslie Shippen had won probation, a stiff fine, and a suspended jail sentence as a first-offender. Evidently he had either been cured, or else his vocational art work had shortly thereafter begun to flourish, because he had nothing more on his record, and the race-track interlude had been seven years earlier.

The FBI had nothing more than that, and as the clerk in Files and Records told Alvarado, in his line of work where he dealt with the worst side of human nature day in, day out, for years, someone with *that* kind of a record was as pure as the driven snow.

Maybe. To George Alvarado, a demonstration of criminality in people, once they got out of their teens, and regardless of how respectable they might have become in later years, still suggested that they had larceny in their hearts. Seven years was a long time, only in the sense that Shippen had been making plenty of money legitimately for that period of time; more, perhaps, than he could have made by forging racetrack tickets — or he would have stayed with the forging business.

In fact, the image of Leslie Shippen

Inspector Alvarado was knocking together from bits and pieces, was of a man who was perhaps not downright villainous, but who was a little left of being a church pillar. Not that it mattered one bit to George Alvarado. In fact, for his purposes, it would please him to discover that Shippen *was* involved in something illegal. *Someone* had to have been sufficiently incensed at Shippen to want him dead, and if that someone turned out to be involved in something illegal, it would make things much simpler for George Alvarado.

Shippen was shaping up as an average human being; average in the sense that he was not an ethical person, but was just exactly as honest as the law required him to be. In Alvarado's work, this was the type of citizen most often encountered, either as an offender, or as a complainant. Felonious types were George Alvarado's bread-and-butter, the devious, sneaky, underhanded and unethical types, were more commonplace, and hence more often encountered, but, like Leslie Shippen, they were probably law-breakers only when they had to be, not because they really *wanted* to be.

There was, of course, one un-average thing about Leslie Shippen: a lethal knife wound.

Alvarado went back to his study of the model lists, and even telephoned two of the agencies shown on Shippen's scribbled notes. He did not know quite what to expect, but it did not take long for him to learn what he was going to get each time he mentioned Leslie Shippen's name.

Evidently Shippen had used many different girls, paid well and promptly, and was not too exacting. The mention of his name wrought an immediate change in the voice of the model agents. Those voices changed still again, after George Alvarado had identified himself, identified his bureau — Homicide — and stated that he was calling in reference to models used recently by the late Leslie Shippen.

He did not mention one particular girl, the one in the magnificent oil portrait in Shippen's studio. He had another plan for her. What he asked for, and got, from the agencies, was the name and telephone number of the girls who had posed for Shippen within the past couple of months.

He spent the entire afternoon telephoning those girls, his feet propped atop the desk, his tie askew, his jacket hanging on the wall, the window open at his back to permit a delightfully fragrant springtime breeze to come through, and all those fascinating, sultry voices of beautiful models coming down the telephone line to him, yielded practically nothing.

After a while he developed a routine. He would ask about the work, about Shippen as a man, and about other girls who had worked for him. In this manner he learned that Shippen did not expect the models to indulge in extra-curricular callisthenics with him, personally, while at the studio-apartment, but now and then he would offer a fringe benefit or two — supper, dancing, the theatre — if a girl appealed to him.

Alvarado also learned, by this cross-questioning system of identical interrogation, that almost every model knew of a girl named Elisabeth Fraser who posed for serious art work for Leslie Shippen several times a year. But that's all they knew of her, and they knew that much simply because, when they had admired something he'd done of Elisabeth Fraser, he had mentioned her name. He had never done any more than that.

But Alvarado did not worry. He doggedly dialled away most of the afternoon, perfectly confident that if Elisabeth Fraser were a professional model, she would have an agent.

It only uneasily entered his mind by four o'clock that, just possibly, the magnificent woman in the fresh portrait was *not* a professional model, or, if she *were*, that she was some kind of very exclusive, self-employed model, because none of the agencies nor agents he talked to had an Elisabeth Fraser on their books.

It was almost five o'clock, quitting time, when Alvarado took his coat off the wall, pocketed a polaroid camera, and went down to his car for the drive back to Palm Drive, and the Shippen studio.

He took four photographs of the nude,

allowed them to develop then and there, and when he was quite satisfied, he pocketed them, and went downstairs, where he was met by a pleasant-faced, nearly bald man in his later years, who introduced himself as the manager, and Alvarado tried one of the photographs on this individual.

The manager gazed a long time at the picture. In fact he was still standing like a stone statue looking at the photograph, when Alvarado said, 'Well . . . ?'

'Oh yes,' replied the manager, handing back the photograph. 'Yes indeed, I've seen her go up to the studio lots of times.'

'You didn't seem that certain, a moment ago,' said Alvarado, and got a predictable reply. 'Oh, yes, I was certain the moment I saw her face. But I never saw her without any clothes on before. She is beautiful. I always thought so. Magnificent woman. But without any clothes . . . '

Alvarado cleared his throat. 'Did you by any chance ever hear her name?'

'No,' replied the older man. 'No, I never heard her name. Mr. Shippen never

mentioned the girls he used in his work
. . . I presume he used them in his work,
he *was* an artist. If I'd ever thought . . . '

'He used them in his work,' stated
Alvarado. 'When was the last time you
saw this woman arrive here, and go up to
the studio?'

The manager pondered a moment
before replying. 'It was probably about a
week ago. But she could have gone up
after that. You see, I belong to a bowling
league, and this past week we've been in a
city-wide tournament, so I've been away
much of the time.'

'But perhaps your wife saw . . . ?'

'I have no wife. Sorry.'

Alvarado sighed. 'Great.' His one hope
for a witness to the arrival or departure of
Elisabeth Fraser on the day Leslie
Shippen was murdered, was just ruined
by a bowling ball.

Then the manager redeemed himself a
little. 'She drives a very attractive small,
foreign car. Blue, with red upholstery. She
keeps it as clean as a pin. It is always
shiny.'

She *had* been at the studio-apartment

the day Shippen had been killed, then. Alvarado thanked the manager and started down towards his car at the kerbing. The manager allowed him to get part way, then called, and ambled down into the tree-shade where Alvarado had halted and turned back.

He gave Alvarado a slightly quizzical look. 'Aren't you going to interrogate me about Mr. Shippen's other visitors?'

George, jacket slung over his shoulder, became resigned, but as a matter of fact any other visitors Shippen might have had *last week*, when the manager had been around, were only going to be important if any of them turned up during the course of an interrogation of Elisabeth Fraser, and *that* was what Alvarado had in mind at the moment, a long talk with the full-bodied, long-legged, exquisite woman with the old-coppery hair.

He liked to keep his cases as uncomplicated as he could. 'If Mr. Shippen had any *particular* visitors,' he said, and let it hang like that in the air.

The manager said, 'Women. Inspector, Les Shippen had more women call on

50

him, and I mean *women*, if you know what I mean, than any one man had a right to.'

George knew exactly what the manager meant. He had seen the way the older man had stood ogling that picture of the oil portrait.

'Aside from the girl in the picture, did he have any special woman call on him?' Alvarado asked. 'Or did you ever get the impression he might be really involved with a particular woman?'

The manager returned Alvarado's gaze without blinking, then he said, 'That's the hell of it, Inspector. He seemed to treat them all the same.' The manager's round, faintly perspiring face showed disgust. 'Can you imagine having naked women all over your studio, like *he* had, and not getting involved?'

Alvarado blew out a big breath, glanced at his wrist, and cut this short. 'I'll be back,' he told the older man. 'Right now I'm a little pressed for time, but I'll be back and we'll talk again.' He smiled, bobbed his head, and made his escape.

5

A Little Encouragement

The following morning he did not arrive at his office until shortly before noon, and the reason was elemental; he had gone directly from his apartment to the first four of those model agencies he'd contacted the day before, and displayed his photographs of the Elisabeth Fraser nude.

He had drawn sighs of appreciation, perhaps for the art work, but he thought the sighs were for something else because each agent he showed the photograph to was male, but he did not come up with anything at all about a model named Elisabeth Fraser.

He was annoyed, but a long way from despairing, by the time he got back to the office. If Elisabeth Fraser *without* her clothes on, was un-identifiable, *with* her clothes on, she was liable to identification by just about every public agency in the state, or in the nation. As it turned out, Alvarado did not have to go to the national level, for although Files and Records had nothing on anyone named Elisabeth Fraser, the Division of Motor Vehicles, up in Sacramento, which had charge of every motor vehicle operator's licence in the State of California, not only had seven Elisabeth Frasers, four of whom resided in the Los Angeles area, but it also had copies of those small face-on photographs which were a part of every car-driver's licensing permit.

Alvarado duly mailed one of his polaroid photos to Sacramento, then went out to a late lunch, and when he returned, ran into Captain Murphy, who asked about progress. They entered Alvarado's office to confer. Captain Murphy was interested in Elisabeth Fraser, but he was more interested in a motive for the Shippen killing, and on this score Alvarado had nothing, not even any ideas.

Captain Murphy was sympathetic. 'Something will turn up. You and I have been in this business too long to think otherwise.'

Alvarado was sardonic. 'Yeah, that's what I'm afraid of. Something will turn up, to make it victim number five.'

Murphy fatuously shoved that aside. 'What is to be will be. There's something that bothers me, George: Where is the connection between an affluent artist in Beverly Hills, and three beaners on the other side of the city?'

Alvarado's answer to that was brusque. 'If I knew that, Captain, I'd have a fair idea about the person I'm after.'

Murphy said he'd done a little investigating on his own. 'Within the building, you understand; not trying to muscle in on your assignment, George, just curious. But those four men had nothing in common. I had some idea it might be a fatal rip-off from perhaps a narcotics feud — something like that. It wasn't. In fact, the more I delved the more it looked to me as though it's the work of a nut, some guy running around in the city committing pointless homicides.'

Alvarado could have agreed, but, as he now said, whether the killer was simply a deranged homicidal maniac, or not, he still had to be caught, and of course Captain Murphy agreed. Then he departed, which permitted Alvarado to resume his work.

It occurred to him to make a personal search for the women named Elisabeth Fraser, known to be living in the Los Angeles area. If there were only four of them, and the Department of Motor Vehicles had the address of each woman, it shouldn't be difficult to find all four, and perhaps limit it to the one in particular who was a model.

He did not make the effort. A man named Sorenson, an executive in a Los Angeles bank branch, called in and was routed to Alvarado from the Booking and Information desk, who said he had been following the fire ant killing in the newspaper, and had a little personal knowledge of the latest victim, Leslie Shippen.

Shippen had an account with the outlying branch-bank where Sorenson was an official. Three days before his death, Leslie Shippen had made a sizable withdrawal, six thousand dollars in cash, and Sorenson was wondering if the police knew about this. He was also wondering if perhaps that money might not have had something to do with Shippen's murder.

Sorenson's theory was that Shippen's demise had something to do with either blackmail or perhaps robbery.

Alvarado ruled out robbery without saying so, and asked Sorenson how large an account Shippen had had at the bank.

'That was it,' stated the bank officer. 'Six thousand; when he withdrew that he depleted the account. But he didn't close out the account, which is customary when people withdraw all their funds. My theory is that although he cleaned out the account, he did not do so with the intention of concluding his business with the bank. Otherwise, he'd have closed out the account. It would seem as though he had to pay someone that money. I went over his deposit and withdrawal record this morning. He added to the account over a period of months, and only very rarely made any withdrawals, which is also customary with a savings account, and his withdrawals were small — never more than a couple of hundred dollars at a time.'

Alvarado had a question. 'How about a checking account?'

'Not with our branch,' replied Sorenson. 'But he surely had one, somewhere. If you wish, I can institute a search, within our bank.'

Alvarado agreed that this might prove useful, then he asked Sorenson also to ascertain, if he could, whether some other customer had made a six-thousand-dollar deposit within a period beginning three days before Shippen's murder, and three or four days afterwards. To this the banker agreed, saying that such a search might take several days since the bank was quite large and had more than forty branch-banks in Los Angeles County.

Alvarado was interested in how long this might take. and when Sorenson said possibly three or four days, Alvarado was satisfied.

After he had noted Sorenson's full

name, telephone number and home address, he rang off, and for a while he sat at his desk staring at the wall, running through his mind the reasons he had encountered in his police career, for people to withdraw large sums of money from their bank accounts. He was inclined towards a feeling that blackmail was involved, but that did not stand up very well when he speculated about the three dead *Chicanos*, who had all been labourers. Still, to test this, he telephoned several banks in the *Chicano* district to ascertain whether Holquin, Mendez or Gomez, had savings accounts. It was not uncommon, of course, but it was not very probable either, not in an era of national inflation, when wage-workers were the first to feel the pinch.

He got a surprise. All three of the dead *Chicanos* had had bank accounts. What was more intriguing, all three had made large withdrawals shortly before they had been killed. But only one of them, Holquin, had withdrawn all his money.

Alvarado, sensing at last the connection he so badly needed, made a formal request for the deposit and withdrawal records of those three dead men.

Then he tried to imagine why anyone would blackmail three labourers. It was not unusual, and obviously it was entirely plausible, that Mendez, Holquin and Gomez had done something which would make them liable to blackmail; labourers, particularly those working in construction, had opportunities to steal material, fixtures, articles of value with a re-sale potential. It happened every day, somewhere in the city.

But if this were behind those first three murders, then the implication was that someone else in the building trade was the blackmailer — and there certainly was no visible connection between three construction labourers, and a successful artist-illustrator.

But there *was* a connection. The more Alvarado thought about it the more convinced he became. He also thought it probable that the three *Chicanos* and the successful artist had to have known one another, had at least to have crossed paths, somehow.

But with all three of the *Chicanos* dead, along with Leslie Shippen, any worthwhile source for this possible connection was beyond Alvarado's reach. He could have gone to interrogate the survivors of Holquin, Mendez and Gomez, but he didn't. If something illegal had been going on, the dead men would not very likely have confided in their wives or parents.

Perhaps, in time, Alvarado would have to call upon the survivors of those three men, but for the present he was more interested in establishing the fact that they, and Leslie Shippen, had followed an identical banking pattern.

He spent the balance of the day working up backgrounds on the three dead *Chicanos*, where they had worked, for which construction outfits, what their particular specialities had been, what their wage-scale had been, and although there were inescapable similarities, it still came out that none of those men had worked on the same jobs, or had seemed to know one another. He also came up with the riddle of day-labourers being able to have savings accounts, in an era when it took just about every penny men like that could make, just to feed families and keep roofs over their heads.

This did not apply with respect to Leslie Shippen, who had been adequately successful to have a legitimate savings account, but still, the connection, tenuous though it appeared to be, *was* there, and whether it made any sense or not, George Alvarado was encouraged by its existence. It did not constitute the affinity he needed in order to establish a motive for murder, but, riddle or not, it at least gave him something to use as his investigative base.

He telephoned Charles Fisk at the coroner's office because he was certain Leslie Shippen's post mortem had probably been concluded, and Fisk confirmed that Shippen's post had indeed been accomplished, the report which was to be forwarded to the police was in process of being prepared — and there was no question at all about the fact that the same knife, with the small chips in its cutting-edge, had been used.

That clinched it for Alvarado. He'd had no doubts, but police work throve only on hard evidence.

He closed his desk for the day, ambled out of the building and across the street to the cafe where he, and most other police-bachelors, ate, had some coffee and wasted three-quarters of an hour talking to an officer from the bunco squad, not about anything in particular, but about police work, which was what all policemen discussed when they came together. The man from bunco noted unhappily that crime, in all categories, was on the increase, not just in Los Angeles, but throughout the entire state, a theme George Alvarado was tired of listening to, but this evening he listened, he even commiserated with the detective from bunco.

Later, by the time he got to his flat, showered, took a glass of beer to the sitting room where he got comfortable for the evening newscast on television, he had forgotten most of what the detective from the bunco squad had said, and was back again, mentally picking away at his private riddle of four men knifed to death by someone the *Chicano* press had dubbed the fire ant, and who was now referred to by that name in all the city newspapers.

The news was bad, as usual, perhaps a little worse this evening than usual, because, aside from all the cruelty indulged in by people throughout the world, Nature had joined in with two devastating tornados in the southern states, and a great tidal wave had struck Japan, making it appear that even Nature was going amok.

Alvarado finished his beer, switched channels, got a night baseball game, decided it was worth watching, and padded barefoot out to the kitchen for another beer. Baseball was a game that traditionally required spectators to drink beer.

Finally, by the time he was drowsy enough to retire, he could forget his assignment, which is what he had been trying to do since the first beer. The Department pyschologists had been saying for years that police officers should never take their work home with them, which was probably good advice, but it was rather like telling a man in a rainstorm that he should avoid the risk of getting wet because he might catch pneumonia. Everyone knew what people *should* do, they just did not have very many satisfactory methods for them to follow in order to survive the strain of everyday living.

When Alvarado retired, his last thought was of the portrait in Shippen's studio of Elisabeth Fraser. It was certainly a worthwhile reflection for a single man to go to sleep thinking about.

6

A Blue MG

Despite the banker's prediction, the day before, that three or four days would be required to ferret up all the information about a depositor putting six thousand dollars into an account within the span of time allowed by Alvarado, for this kind of a search, Sorenson was on the telephone before ten o'clock the next morning with a list of names, account numbers, and city addresses, of a number of people who had deposited precisely six thousand dollars with Sorenson's bank within the critical period.

Sorenson read off the names, gave the pertinent information, and George Alvarado copied it all down at his desk.

The list was by no means complete, according to the bank. For that, several more days would inevitably be required, but Sorenson thought that if the police started investigating the people on the incomplete list, today, by the time the balance of the names could be supplied, the police would have gone a long way towards eliminating the innocent.

Alvarado sighed, thanked the banker, put down the telephone, and briefly reflected upon the demonstrable fact that everyone was a detective. He then called the *Chicano* branch-bank for precise information upon the accounts of Gomez, Holquin and Mendez, and this took the better part of an hour to get. Not because the records were obscure, nor even because the bank was reluctant to give confidential information over the tele-phone, even to the police, but the difficulty arose from the fact that deposits and withdrawals had not been brought current in some time.

Alvarado scratched his head over that. He knew nothing of banking, but he *did* know there were banking procedures prescribed by law in the State of California — and presumably throughout the nation — which required efficiency. Perhaps a branch-bank in the *Chicano* community of Los Angeles suffered from the identical shoulder-shrugging-indifference and laxity which marked Mex-town, in general.

In the end, though, he got all those postings, the deposits, and the withdrawals. Then he rang off, leaned to study what he had, and came up with an interesting observation. All three of the *Chicanos* had followed pretty much the same pattern Leslie Shippen had followed. They had deposited much more than they had withdrawn — up to a point — then they had all made sizable withdrawals. But only Holquin and Shippen had withdrawn *all* the funds from their savings accounts.

This did not remain true of checking accounts, however. Both Gomez and Mendez had practically emptied their checking accounts, and within a couple of days of one another.

Alvarado threw down his pencil and went back to stand by the window looking out over acres of unhandsome rooftops.

It was there — the affinity — he just

67

could not put his finger on it. Whatever was similar among those four dead men, was also very *dis*-similar.

The telephone rang. It was the civil servant up in Sacramento, in the Department of Motor Vehicles, Alvarado had spoken to earlier. The man up north had just received a copy of the portrait of Elisabeth Fraser, and his first remark was predictable.

'Man, I don't blame you for going all out in your effort to find *this* lady.'

Alvarado, becoming resigned to this identical reaction every time, simply said, 'Yeah.' Then he said, 'Any luck?'

'Sure,' stated the up-state DVM employee. 'She lives in Beverly Hills.' He gave an address that stunned Alvarado. 'She owns a red and blue MG.' The clerk also gave the licence number of the vehicle. When Alvarado thanked him, the clerk then said, 'Listen, Inspector, if she ever comes up to Sacramento, I could sure show her the town.'

Alvarado gently put down the telephone, studied the information on his lined tablet, then slowly arose, ripped the page from the tablet, pocketed it, and went down to his car.

There was a slight, incoming overcast above the southwesterly regions of the city, this morning. It could presage rainfall, which was not very likely this time of year, or it could presage a combination of sea-fog and city-smog, in which case there would be a cooling trend, which smelled of onions, irritated the eyes and throat, and would probably drive holidayers to the countryside in herds.

Alvarado did not pay much attention. There were many things an adaptable human-being accepted in stride, and the variables of Los Angeles weather was one of them. He drove out to the handsome apartment building where Shippen's studio was, parked down several doors in his unmarked car, and alighted to briefly stand, scanning the parked vehicles up in front of the Shippen-building. By all rights, the blue MG with the red leather upholstery should have been there. It wasn't; Alvarado started back, but when he was abreast of the drive way, he veered off, hiked through to the rear of the building — and there was the little blue MG, secure in a car-port.

He went back round front, sought out the manager's apartment, only half expected to find the balding man at home, and when the manager answered the door, recognised Alvarado and stepped forth smiling, Alvarado said, 'When I was here the other day, you admired that photograph of the beautiful nude girl. Remember?'

The balding man nodded. 'How could I forget?'

Alvarado leaned on the wall, gazing at the older man. 'But you didn't know her.'

'I told you I'd seen her. I said . . . '

'Yeah. I remember all you said,' stated Alvarado. 'Just tell me why you worked so damned hard at creating the impression you could not help me find her — when she lives right here, in this building, in the north wing, and you knew her name, knew where she lived, knew probably more than almost anyone around here, about her?'

The balding man's expression congealed. He did not look chagrined, guilty, nor even actually very uncomfortable about being caught in his big lie, but he *did* look pained as he replied.

'She needed the extra time, so I got it for her. That's all, Inspector. If you want to arrest me for something — obstructing justice? — go right ahead.'

Alvarado continued to lean there, studying the manager. 'Why?' he asked, and the answer was his second stunner for the day.

'Because she is my daughter.'

Alvarado digested this, straightened up off the wall and said, 'Your name on the mailbox, is Albert Knowland — not Fraser.'

'She was married to a man named Fraser when she was sixteen, Inspector. She was divorced from him when she was eighteen. It's a long story, and not a very happy one, if you'd like all the details.'

Alvarado didn't want the details, not right at this time, at any rate. 'Where is she now?' he asked, and the balding man's steady stare did not waver when the answer came.

'I'm sorry, Inspector. I'm not going to tell you where she is.'

'Mind telling me *why* you're not going to tell me that, Mr. Knowland?'

'Because her life is in danger.'

Alvarado had expected this. 'Mr. Knowland, if someone wants to find her, has it occurred to you, that, since you're obviously her confidant, her father, the same person who might want to harm her, just damned well might drive up here, in a day or two, and *make* you tell him where she's hiding — then there would be two casualties, wouldn't there? You *and* your daughter.'

'I have a weapon in the house, Inspector. I'm taking every . . . '

Alvarado interrupted with a head-shake. 'There is no way to take every precaution against the kind of killer you're going up against. They call him the fire ant.'

'That's silly, Inspector, downright ridiculous. It sounds like something some little boys in a tree-house would imagine.'

Alvarado said, 'There are four dead

men to suggest that, ridiculous or not, you and I had better damned well take the fire ant seriously. Now then — you've got a choice; come with me under arrest for obstructing justice, and a couple of other charges I can think of, or co-operate with me so that between us we may be able to keep Elisabeth Fraser alive — and also catch a murderer. It's entirely up to you.'

The older man did not hesitate. Clearly, he had done a lot of thinking about all this, and it was also clear that he was not a man who was easily frightened. He looked Alvarado in the eye and said, 'You're not going to catch a murderer. You're not even going to come close to him, Inspector. But if you ever *do* catch him, you're still not going to be able successfully to prosecute him. Not the way the law is nowadays. For these reasons, I am not going to help you. Am not going to involve myself in any way, in this matter . . . As for Les Shippen, I'm not going to say anything about him one way or the other. He is dead, and that ends it.'

Alvarado said, 'I thought most men as old as you are, had more sense than you've got. All right, stick your head back in the sand.'

The older man's forehead slowly curled up with a broad scowl. 'You are not going to arrest me?'

'If you'll answer just one small question, Mr. Knowland, I won't arrest you. At least I won't arrest you today. The question is: 'Did she see the murderer?''

The older man promptly shook his head. 'No. She was getting dressed in another part of the apartment. Their sitting was only for a half hour that morning. The portrait was finished, to all intents and purposes. Les just had a couple of small touch-ups to do, he told her. She was getting dressed . . . she did not know anyone else had even entered the apartment, until she walked out — and there he was, in a pool of blood.'

'She came down here and telephoned the police, then?'

'No. She went to her own apartment, which is around back, above the car-ports. She called the police from there.

Then she came round here and told me what was up there, in Shippen's studio. We talked, and she ran out front, got into her car and drove away.'

Alvarado studied the older man for a moment, nodded and without another word, walked away. He had picked up a very strong probability, and wanted to check it out. When he got back to his parked car, he called in for a surveillance team, gave a description of Albert Knowland, and the blue MG sports car, and cruised back down to Wilshire Boulevard, on his way back to the office, except that he did not return, instead, he had a very leisurely luncheon at a kosher delicatessen, studied the hands of his watch, finally returned to his vehicle, and called in.

The man answering Knowland's description as given to the surveillance team had only moments before led his plainclothesmen-shadows to a private residence on Sorrel Lane, and he had driven a handsome little blue MG car all the way.

Alvarado's suspicion about Albert

Knowland not owning a car, and therefore having to use his daughter's car, had paid off. Alvarado released the surveillance team, drove round a residential square to head in the direction of Sorrel Lane, and shook his head.

Albert Knowland might be a brave, admirably loyal parent, but he sure as hell was a stupid individual when it came to being prudent. Anyone with the intelligence God had given a goose, could have done exactly what Alvarado had done — the difference being that Alvarado was not a fire ant.

When he hauled up down the block ten or fifteen yards from the residence on Sorrel Lane, he was impressed. It was an old house, in the traditional Spanish tradition of architecture which had once prevailed through Beverly Hills — all Southern California, for the matter of that — and it was set back within the confines of a beautifully landscaped large plot of ground. As Alvarado strolled up the sidewalk in tree-shade, he wondered who owned this obviously very expensive piece of real estate. A man who managed an apartment building obviously would not be able to afford anything like this, and a girl who posed for artists would not be able to afford it, either. Alvarado had no actual knowledge of the value of the magnificent old house and its lovely grounds, but he did not have to possess that kind of knowledge to realise, just from looking around as he walked towards the shaded patio and the hand-carved oaken front door of the house, that this kind of an estate would cost more to purchase, than most people made in many, many years.

7

An Old Trick Works

The balding, older man who opened the door and stood in stunned immobility gazing out at George Alvarado was the same man Inspector Alvarado had spoken to about an hour and a half earlier, Albert Knowland.

Alvarado seized the initiative. 'It's nice in the shade of the patio, but it would be better if we talked inside.'

The older man shot a sudden look over his shoulder, then stepped aside for Alvarado to step into the cool, shadowy large sitting room.

Alvarado saw the girl in the archway between the sitting room and the beamed, sunken big dining room which was adjoining. He nodded gravely, thinking that she was, if possible, even more beautiful than her portrait.

'Mrs. Fraser,' he murmured, and

offered a crooked little smile. 'I'm the snoopy detective your father was just telling you about.'

She was not as surprised, nor as slow to recover, as her father was. She smiled back and said, 'He under-estimated you.'

Alvarado shrugged, motioned for her father to close the door, then turned slowly to gaze around. The interior of the charming old house was very tastefully — and very expensively — furnished according to the architecture, with massive old carved pieces of furniture. As Alvarado finished his inspection, with more actual appreciation, in view of his personal background, than most people would have felt, he fixed a sardonic stare upon the older man.

'There were cars in all but two of the ports out back of the apartment-building, Mr. Knowland. One of those ports went to an apartment with no name over the mailbox, signifying there was no occupant for that apartment. The other empty car-port was behind your ground floor flat, suggesting that you did not own a car. So — you drove the blue MG, and were followed.' Alvarado looked at the girl again. 'Would you come in here and sit down and join us, please?'

She kept watching Alvarado, still showing more poise than her father; in fact, she looked almost as though she might really smile, but instead, she strolled to a chair, sat, and raised her greeny gaze to her father as she said, 'It's all right. Well; at least it happened, and that's not going to be changed, is it?'

The older man finally crossed to a chair and eased down. For the first time, he looked actually chagrined. Alvarado saw the expression and said, 'I told you, a couple of hours ago, that if someone really wanted to find her, they'd do it. Just be thankful it was not someone else, Mr. Knowland.' He faced the beautiful woman. 'If you weren't involved in what happened to Leslie Shippen, why did you run?'

The greeny gaze did not waver. 'Inspector, I ran because I was afraid. I have no idea who came in and killed Les Shippen. That's all I could have told the police if I'd stayed and waited. That's all I can tell you, now. I was dressing in the bedroom. I didn't even hear anyone at the door. When I came out — he was on the floor, with blood all around him. I've only seen one other dead person in my life, that was after an auto accident three years ago on the freeway, but you *feel* death, more than you *see* it. I knew, after one look, that Les was dead. There was no one else in the studio. The door was half open. I left, went to my apartment, called the police, ran down to my father's apartment, told him, then I went out, got into my car, just as a police car drew up behind me, and I drove over here. That's everything I can tell you.'

Alvarado, studying the beautiful woman, gauging her as he listened, now said, 'That's not quite all you can tell me, Mrs. Fraser. For example — why did it occur to you to flee so suddenly and swiftly? What was there in the back of your mind, when you saw Shippen dead on the floor, that made you want to get away from him, from his apartment, even from the building where he lived, so swiftly? *What did you know about Leslie Shippen that made you react like that, so spontaneously?'*

The girl was quiet for a moment. She understood Alvarado's implication. She relaxed slightly, settled back more comfortably in her chair, and turned a long look upon her father. Finally she said, 'I think you're probably quite good at your trade, Inspector.' She turned back to face him. 'I sat for Leslie Shippen quite often. He said I was the best model he'd ever employed. And that's what it was, employment.'

'And . . . ?'

'Well; it's impossible not to learn a little about someone you're around a good bit of the time, isn't it? Leslie Shippen was a complicated man, Inspector. He — he was involved in something besides his art. Twice in the past couple of months while we were working, he received telephone calls, and immediately cancelled our sitting to rush out and drive away.'

Her father started to interrupt, but the girl ignored this and said, 'Two weeks ago, when the portrait we'd been working on most recently, was nearly finished, a man called at the studio. Leslie went to the door, looked out, said something to the man, then, holding the door almost completely closed, turned and told me to go into the bedroom and get dressed. I went. While I was getting dressed I heard them raise their voices. When I was dressed and came out, Leslie was sitting at his desk, alone. He didn't even glance up as he handed me an envelope with my fee in it, which was how he paid me, after each sitting, and told me he'd call me when we'd sit again.'

'That's all?' asked Alvarado.

'Yes, that's all. Except that he didn't call me for several days.' Elisabeth Fraser turned again towards her father. Albert Knowland said, 'Mr. Shippen was gone for two days; he did not return at night, either. He did not return until the third day.'

Alvarado walked to a sofa and sank down, gazing from the father to the daughter. 'From this, then, you deduced that Leslie Shippen was possibly involved in something illegal.'

'Well,' said the girl, 'perhaps something a little shady, Inspector. Not necessarily illegal, but perhaps a little — strange.'

'And that's why you fled when you found him dead?'

She nodded.

Alvarado sat in thoughtful silence for a moment, his gaze lingering on the beautiful woman. Finally, he asked her a question. 'Did he always pay you in cash?'

'Yes, and it was always in an envelope. He usually had the envelope lying atop the desk when I arrived, so he had to have counted it out and put it in the envelope before I arrived.' She hesitated, then added a little more to this. 'That's not an unusual procedure, Inspector, in my line of work.'

Alvarado smiled. 'I don't know very much about your line of work, Mrs. Fraser, so I'll be grateful for a little guidance as we go along. Tell me; do you model for other artists?'

'Yes, but only on a private basis.'

'And how did Shippen happen to contact you?'

'By accident, Inspector. We met in the patio of my father's apartment building, got into a conversation, and when he told me he was an artist, I told him I was a model. That's all there was to it. He asked me to sit for him a few days later, and from then on I worked for him quite often.' She pointed to a portrait upon the front wall of the sitting room, which had been hidden by the door when Alvarado had first entered the house. 'He did that portrait of me.'

It was a very good partial profile; it showed Elisabeth Fraser in a mood of gentle, scarcely discernible poignancy. It was a little haunting. Alvarado gazed at it, then leaned a little to gaze closer. Elisabeth Fraser, watching his reaction, said, 'Do you like it?'

Alvarado nodded. 'Very much. He was talented, wasn't he?'

She lifted her face to the portrait when she replied. 'I think he was probably one of the most talented artists I've ever known.'

Alvarado, still studying the portrait in its half-light, half-shadow, slowly inclined his head. 'Coming from you, that would be a real compliment.' He turned slowly back to her. 'Did he say he got good money for his work?'

She answered quietly, 'I never asked, and he never said. When you're sitting, Inspector, you don't keep up a conversation.'

Alvarado accepted the mild rebuke. 'Well, as I said, I don't know much about artists.'

Her face softened a little. 'His work will probably become fairly valuable now. At least, that's how it works, sometimes, if an artist was superior, and he certainly was; when they die, and there are only a limited number of their paintings around, the value seems to increase. Leslie's art was also his therapy. Did you go over his apartment, Inspector?'

'Yes.'

'Did you see the stacked paintings in the closet off his bedroom?'

'Yes.'

'That's where he put the pieces he liked most.'

Alvarado looked from the portrait to the girl. 'Then he didn't sell much of his work.'

She returned Alvarado's steady gaze in

a thoughtful manner, before replying. 'I guess not. I suppose that would be the answer to your earlier question, about him selling his art, wouldn't it?'

Alvarado did not answer one way or the other way. He arose, shot another glance at the portrait, then turned towards Elisabeth Fraser's father. 'I'd like you to tell me something, Mr. Knowland.'

The older man raised his eyes, warily and defensively.

'You want to protect your daughter. I don't blame you for that one bit. Now tell me, Mr. Knowland, whether you think you're capable of doing it? Do you know how easy it was for me to find her here? I did it while eating lunch in a kosher delicatessen.'

'But you're the police,' protested the older man.

Alvarado gently shook his head. 'The police aren't the only ones who have people trained to hunt down fugitives. They are the only ones who hunt down people either to arrest them for obstructing justice, or to put them into protective custody. The others who hunt people down, very often do it to shut them up, permanently. I'm not saying anyone is going to do this to your daughter, especially if the fire ant, whoever he is, doesn't know she was in Shippen's apartment when Shippen was killed, but I *will* say that when the coroner holds his inquest, and your daughter is subpoenaed as the only known person who *might* have had a chance to see the fire ant, she's going to be in danger — and I don't think you're qualified to protect her. Not if the way you attempted it today is an indication of your ability in this direction.'

Elisabeth Fraser, watching Alvarado as he spoke to her father, came up with a question. 'And you have a solution, Inspector?'

He turned. 'It's not so much a solution, Mrs. Fraser, as it's what I get paid for. Both of you should go back to the precinct station with me.' He offered her his little rueful smile again. 'I could arrest your father for obstructing justice, and hold him overnight, I suppose, but I don't really have a valid excuse for arresting you, and actually, you're the one who needs the protective custody. In any case, you can both have an attorney spring you within a half hour of being booked, which means, Mrs. Fraser, you'll be out on the street again.'

The greeny eyes darkened slightly. 'You're suggesting I'll be in danger when I'm freed.'

'No, I'm not suggesting anything. But the minute the newspapers read the booking report, and pick up your name as someone involved in the Shippen case, and publish it for the reading public, if the fire ant thinks you might be a real threat to him — there is no question in my mind that you'll be in danger.'

The beautiful woman turned slightly towards her father. 'We discussed this, didn't we?'

The older man, who looked every year of his age right at this moment, replied roughly. 'But I had no idea they'd come in this fast.'

Elisabeth Fraser arose, turning an ironic gaze upon George Alvarado. 'I think you've just been complimented,

Inspector. Well; am I under arrest?'

Alvarado's answer surprised them both. 'No. Just let me use your telephone, and I'll arrange for protection to be sent out for you, right here. Incidentally, who owns this house?'

Albert Knowland answered. 'I do. I've owned it for thirty years. This is where my daughter grew up. Why did you ask?'

Alvarado simply said, 'It's delightful. Now, if you'll show me where the telephone is, please . . . ?'

8

Little Bingo!

By nature Gerald Murphy was not a sceptic, but as he sat listening to George Alvarado, he gave a believable performance of scepticism. 'You just left her sitting out there?' he asked, and Alvarado answered a trifle wryly.

'I suppose you could say that, except that she had two plainclothesmen from the downstairs rookie division patrolling the grounds, her father is with her most of the time, and I told her specifically not to unlock a door or a window, and not to go outside unless someone is with her . . . Captain, we're taking all those precautions, and the fire ant doesn't even know who she is, or why we're keeping her under tight security.'

Murphy said, 'I don't know, either, George. Yeah, I understood what you said a minute ago — she was in the flat when

Shippen got it, but unless you believe she saw something, regardless of what she says, why all these damned expensive precautions?'

'She's my bait, Jerry.'

'Oh.' Murphy pondered this a moment. 'Does she know, did you explain this to her?'

'No. But I will. Jerry, I want everything set up exactly right, first. Then I'll tell her.'

Murphy's simulated scepticism began to look increasingly genuine. 'It's an old ploy, George maybe it won't work. And if it *does* work, maybe it'll work too well.'

Alvarado was nettled. 'Tell me what else to do? It's now been three days since the fire ant hit Leslie Shippen. It's about time for him to hit someone else. We can go along the way we've been going, and let him run up quite a string of scores, or we can do *something*, and at least have a run at him.'

Captain Murphy arose as though to depart, still looking doubtful. 'You do what you think must be done, George, only for gawd's sake try not to get someone killed by this bastard, if you can help it. And one more thing . . . '

'Damn it,' snapped Alvarado, stung by Murphy's last remark, 'I'm the one who's been trying to devise some way to prevent these killings. I don't appreciate that kind of a statement. Jerry, you've sure as hell got the right to take me off this case.'

Captain Murphy's steady pale eyes went to Alvarado's face and remained there. 'You know, George, it was enlightening to me when we went to lunch last week; until then I had no idea you were touchy.' He went to the door. 'I realise you're as interested in preventing these killings as you are in catching the fire ant.' He walked out, and closed the door, and the telephone rang. George scooped it up, still annoyed. The caller was Sorenson, from the branch-bank, with additional names for Alvarado. When this session was concluded, Alvarado sat gazing at his list. The number of people who deposited exactly six thousand dollars for the week during which Leslie Shippen was killed, seemed practically endless. Why so many people should all of a sudden deposit exactly six thousand dollars was a puzzler. At least it was until Alvarado worked out the number of people depositing money in banks around the city, who deposited more, or less, than six thousand dollars, and that included people who deposited in *all* city banks, not just Sorenson's bank, then it looked a lot less unique.

It also looked pretty damned appalling. Alvarado could not possibly run investigations on all those people, without a horde of assistants. He decided to let this pass for the time being, and concentrate on trying to induce the fire ant to come to him, instead of doing as he had been doing up to now, groping through mazes in search of the fire ant.

There were no guarantees, of course, and, as Captain Murphy had implied, there was some danger to his current plan. Well hell, there was danger in crossing a street at high noon, there was danger in stepping into, or out of, a bathtub.

He left the office before noon and drove back to Leslie Shippen's studio again. He did not look for Albert

Knowland, and used his own key to let himself into the apartment. He went directly to that closet in the bedroom where Shippen had stored the paintings he had cherished, and systematically brought most of them forth, placed them face-up on the bed, and even arranged some of them along the wall. Then he crossed to the window, partially closed out the brilliant sunlight, and stood a long while studying Shippen's art, which was actually very good. As Elisabeth Fraser had said, Leslie Shippen was a gifted and talented man. Alvarado also felt inclined to agree with her speculation that his art would now begin to increase in value.

But Alvarado was not an art critic; he did not own a single oil portrait, and excepting several of the Shippen landscapes he was admiring now, the only two paintings he had ever seen he would have offered money for, were both of Elisabeth Fraser, one a nude, the other a hauntingly beautiful portrait of her exquisite face, slightly averted, slightly poignant.

That was not why he was studying the

Shippen art. He had to bring every painting from the closet and line them up like soldiers, before he saw what he had hoped to find.

Evidently Leslie Shippen seldom sold a painting, or, if he did sell very many of them, then he must have been a more prolific painter than Alvarado thought he was.

The unique thing was that although Shippen's illustrations were infinitely more numerous, about all Alvarado found at his apartment were roughed-in work-sheets, stacks of carelessly piled initial sketches, all of them with scrawled notations for proposed changes on the margins, and art work which had been painted over, or altered in some other way, preliminary work.

Apparently Leslie Shippen was more professional with respect to his illustrations. Alvarado got the impression that Shippen was cold-blooded about his illustrations. He ground them out with an impersonal, skilled and prolific professionalism. They obviously were his bread-and-butter. But the oil paintings were his labours of love.

Still, there was a distinctive mark to both varieties of art work. Leslie Shippen art was notable for the distinctive, almost clinically perfect sweep of its lines. Alvarado was ready to concede, after an hour of studying the paintings, and work-sheets of illustrations, that he would be able to identify a Shippen painting or drawing anywhere he saw one.

Using his polaroid camera, he systematically photographed a round dozen of the paintings, and another dozen of the less painstakingly completed work-sheets of Shippen illustrations.

Then he put everything back where he had found it, went out into the studio and spent another hour reading every notation, every letter and scribbled bit of Shippen's handwriting he could find, before departing. He appropriated only two written samples of Leslie Shippen's handwriting, neither one of them important except for the way they demonstrated Shippen's artistic, clean-lined handwriting.

Then he returned to his office, and it

was near the end of the day when he finally decided which of the photographed duplications of Shippen art he wanted reproduced and enlarged, and took them downstairs to the laboratory and left them.

He was passing across in front of Communications when a handsome woman in her thirties, with tight, short curly hair and keen blue eyes, saw him and called. There had been a call for him. He took the note, and returned to his office before returning the call.

Elisabeth Fraser was at the other end of the line. She said, 'Inspector, I know you're busy, but I was wondering if you could stop by, perhaps tomorrow some time. It's nothing important, really; I haven't suddenly remembered anything. It's just that — well — it's hard not to think when you're cooped up like this.'

He smiled at the wall, promised to try and see her, rang off, and sat comfortably loose and easy for a while, before closing his desk for the night, and heading out of the building.

He had dinner near his flat, went home

to follow through on his habitual procedure of showering, watching the nightly newscast on television, with a glass of beer, and later on, he went to bed and slept like a baby, which was in contrast to the way he had slept the previous night.

The following morning he was the first person to visit the lab downstairs, aside from the people employed down there, and although he got a couple of cynical glances from technicians who were accustomed to being nagged and hurried, he also got his enlargements.

He was in his office when Captain Murphy poked his head in, saw Alvarado standing back by the window gazing at the enlargements, and walked on in. As he crossed the small office Captain Murphy glanced at the desk, saw the enlargements of Shippen art, and said, 'Police work is very broadening. After twenty years of it a man has learned to appreciate a whole range of . . . ' Murphy stopped dead still, staring at the enlargements. 'Gawddamn,' he exclaimed, staring hard at a particular painting of three heads, three men standing loosely together against a broad landscape with a rising sun tinting the hills and trees and grass around them.

Alvarado smiled a little. 'Holquin, Mendez and Gomez. The little photograph prints beneath the oil painting, are from our files, from the Department of Motor Vehicles files, actually. Shippen did better with his brush than the DMV cameras did with their lenses.'

Captain Murphy went to the desk and leaned a little. 'Then Shippen *did* know the other three guys the fire ant killed.'

Alvarado nodded. 'Step back, Captain. Don't view oil paintings up close like that.'

Murphy's retort was predictable. 'Oil paintings my tail. I don't give a damn about his talent, George. You've established the connection.'

Alvarado sighed. 'Yeah. They posed for him, and we're damned lucky he never parted with his best oils. They were in a stack of portraits and landscapes in his bedroom closet. What we need now, is to know when Shippen made this painting, and under what circumstances. How did he happen to pick on those three men. Obviously, since what he was portraying was a rural California scene, using men of native descent for authenticity, he would need models like those three — but why Holquin, Mendez and Gomez, and where did he find them?'

Gerald Murphy stepped back slightly. 'Where are the originals?'

'In Shippen's bedroom-closet.'

'You'd better get a court order and bring them in for safekeeping.'

Alvarado did not comment on this, he stepped forward to the desk and pointed to a pair of landscapes. 'I think I know where he painted those. I mean, I think I know those scenes. They're inland, up by the village of Lompoc.' Alvarado pointed to the way he had arranged the paintings. 'See this skyline of backgrounding mountains, Jerry?'

'I'll be damned,' exclaimed the surprised chief of detectives, 'they're contiguous, as though Shippen painted the three men as a sort of close-up, then went on and painted the landscapes in a wider, more distant sweep of rural countryside, from the same place.'

Alvarado turned. 'You're developing into a person with an appreciation of art, Captain.'

'Bull,' exclaimed Murphy. 'I'm a cop who sees something that suggests a damned strong possibility. Okay; so now what will you do — find the place Shippen painted this stuff from?'

Alvarado nodded. 'Maybe Elisabeth Fraser could help me do that.'

Captain Murphy's eyes came up slowly, narrowing on the rise. 'Yeah,' he said in a softly tough voice. 'You be careful about her.' He looked down at the photographic enlargements again, then grunted and headed for the door. Before walking out of the office he shot Alvarado a look. 'Are you going up to Lompoc today? If so, call me at home tonight. I'd like to know what you find up there. Okay?'

Alvarado nodded, leaned to scoop up the enlargements, and after Captain Murphy had departed, Alvarado put all the enlargements into a big manila envelope and took them with him as he headed down for his car.

It was still early in the morning. So early, in fact, that the inundating horde of commuter-traffic hadn't really begun to clog the arterial roadways, yet. He had an almost unimpeded drive out towards Sorrel Lane — with the sun in his eyes almost all the way.

9

An Inadvertent Helper

The plainclothesmen were not in evidence until Alvarado left his car and started across the lawn, then a man appeared from along the north side of the house, and although he probably recognised Inspector Alvarado, he kept right on walking to an interception. He was a young man, but large and thick, and obviously serious when he said, 'Identification!'

Alvarado held out his ID folder, annoyed but also satisfied. 'Where's your partner?' he asked the powerfully-built detective, and got a jerk of the head. 'Round back.'

Alvarado pocketed his folder. 'Anything happening?'

'Dead as the morgue,' stated the younger man. 'How long do you expect to be in there, Inspector?'

Alvarado thought not very long. 'Maybe ten, fifteen minutes.'

The plainclothesman passed Alvarado on by with a curt gesture. He did not smile, and did not stop watching until Alvarado had knocked on the door. Then he retreated back to the north side of the house, and Alvarado shook his head; if the vigilantes were that tough on *him*, what would they be like to someone else?

Elisabeth Fraser was wearing a fawn-coloured, loose-fitting sweater, with slacks of a slightly darker shade. She had her wealth of coppery gold hair in two ponytails, one on each side of her face. She did not look nearly as sophisticated as she had the day before. In fact, she reminded Alvarado of a teen-age school-girl when she stepped aside for him to enter the large, cool house, and smiled up at him.

'I saw the detective stop you,' she said. 'I wasn't sure he'd let you pass.'

Alvarado grinned back. 'I wasn't so sure, either.'

She took him to the sofa he had used yesterday, sat down, and when he sank down too, she studied him a moment before saying, 'I'm wasting your time, aren't I? I mean, just because I'm in limbo doesn't mean you are too, does it?'

He liked her smile. In fact, he liked just about everything about her, but most of all, he liked her lack of ostentation, her poise and her friendly, unaffected personality. He almost said something gallant, but remembered Captain Murphy's admonition in time, and answered differently.

'I'm not in limbo, and you're not wasting my time.' He drew forth the manilla envelope, spread the polaroid photographs upon the coffee table in front of them, and waited for her reaction. It was not immediately forthcoming; she leaned slightly to study the photo enlargements, then finally, she said, 'Leslie's work, isn't it?'

'Yes. You've seen them before?'

She kept studying the photographs as she replied. 'No. But I know his style.' She pointed, tracing out the clean, incisive line where those backgrounding mountains merged with a curving firmament. 'Like an engraving, isn't it? He was so much of a perfectionist.' She looked around. 'Even his illustrations were that — surgical? Would that be the word?'

Alvarado briefly glanced at the pictures, then to her face. 'Don't ask me, Mrs. Fraser. I'm a cop, not an artist. I'm more the comic-book type of art critic.' He sighed. 'I was hoping you'd have seen that landscape in front of you, and the other picture, the one of the three Mexicans.'

She looked down again, gently shaking her head. 'No, but Inspector, he didn't show me much of his work. Oh, he showed me some of his illustrations, but very little of his genuine art. I got the impression, once when we were discussing his work, that he was jealous of his best art. That he painted it for himself, for his own soul-food.' She laughed softly, a little self-consciously. 'I can't draw a dog with a pencil on a piece of wrapping paper, but right now I'm sounding as though I know art. I don't, I only know what appeals to me.'

He smiled. 'Did you ever try to paint?'

She turned large greeny eyes to him. 'Me? Inspector, I'm not aesthetic in any way at all.' Her smile returned, gently. 'Do you know what I do best? Grow vegetables. Out back, right here where I grew up, I used to have a vegetable garden every summer. *That's* my thing.'

They laughed together, then Alvarado admitted that he had no talent either, but in the next breath he returned to the pictures on the coffee table. 'Those three men had to pose for that painting.'

She said, 'Yes. That's clear enough. What of it?' She straightened back a little, eyes narrowing. 'You're looking for those men?'

Alvarado sighed. 'No. I know where they are. What I'd like to know is where Leslie Shippen met them, when he painted them, and what his connection was with them.'

'Well, Inspector, if you know where they are . . . '

'Mrs. Fraser, they are dead.'

She detected something in his tone. 'All three of them?'

'Those were the fire ant's first three victims. Leslie Shippen was his fourth victim. What I'd like to know, is how

Shippen got to know those men. What the circumstances were of their acquaintance-ship.'

Elisabeth Fraser calmly said, 'Have you gone through the modelling agencies?'

Alvarado hadn't, and for a very good reason. Holquin, Gomez and Mendez, were professional labourers, not professional models. 'Waste of time,' he told her. 'They aren't models.'

'In that case, Inspector, did you look in his appointment book? It goes back several years.' She leaned, studied the pictures a moment, then said, 'He probably painted those portraits last winter. This particular shade of ochre with the very faint rusty-gold shade, that exceptionally life-like pastel, is something he developed only about a year ago. He wanted to use it on my nude, but it came out as an incorrect fleshtone for someone of my colouring.'

Alvarado slowly leaned forward, look-ing at the photographs.

Elisabeth Fraser, also leaning, brushed his shoulder as she raised a hand to indicate the particular shading of the three masculine, Latin faces. 'You see; he only used it on this man. The other two are darker, more muddy-tan in facial flesh-tone. Do you see?'

He did not reply until he had picked up the photograph to catch more light on it. Then he answered. 'You're right.' He glanced at her. 'This guy was a real perfectionist, wasn't he?'

She did not answer the question. Instead, she leaned back, saying, 'It's such a tragic waste. Such a thoughtless, pointless, tragic waste. Within another three or four years Leslie's art would have made him very rich.' The greeny eyes lifted, solemnly. 'Even if he didn't seem to care for wealth, I knew him well enough to know he'd have loved the recognition. He used to say no creative person has a right to expect recognition until they are dead. He only made that remark when he was in a rebellious mood. One evening he came to my apartment, after he'd been out in the country somewhere, to ask me to come in for a sitting the next day. He said he'd been far out in the foothills trying to get back in touch with what human existence was all about, and all he'd found had been stupid, vicious humans, and mountains rising from an unfeeling great valley where he was no more important than an ant. He then said that maybe, after he'd been dead ten or twenty years, people would understand what he had been trying so desperately to do — bring therapeutic art to a very ill race of men.'

Alvarado listened, watched the beautiful woman's face, and when she had finished, he said, 'How long ago was that?'

She answered indifferently. 'Oh, about a year ago.'

'And this countryside he was tramping around in, did he say where it was?'

She turned, answering in the same way. 'Inland from the coast, south of Santa Barbara. He mentioned a town but I'd never heard of it and don't remember the . . . '

'Lompoc?'

She stared. 'That's it.' She kept staring. 'How did you know that?'

He arose, picked up the pictures and

slowly placed them back in the manila envelope. He never did answer her question, but he turned, with her still staring at him, and smiled. 'You're really a great help to me, Mrs. Fraser. What you said yesterday, about not knowing anything, isn't true. You're the only real help I've had, so far.'

She went with him to the front door. Over there, as he paused to pocket the envelope, she brushed his arm. 'Yesterday, Inspector, I thought you were basically an uncomplicated man, a dedicated policeman. Today — I'm not so sure of that.'

They stood a moment facing one another, and this time, when the impulse to be gallant came up in him, he yielded to it, regardless of Captain Murphy's warning. 'This doesn't really have anything to do with my work, Mrs. Fraser, but frankly, you sort of — well — you sort of inspire me. You somehow or other create an atmosphere for me that is productive.' He smiled. 'That's pretty crazy, isn't it?' He reached, opened the door, stepped through, and said, 'I'm glad I came out here. I'll be back in a day or two.' He closed the door and started off in the direction of his car. He got as far as the paved walk between his car at the kerbing, and the front of the house, then that massively muscular plain-clothesman strolled over and halted him. From the corner of his eye, Alvarado saw another burly man cross to the front of the house, knock, and when Elisabeth Fraser opened the door, the stocky man on the patio turned, and nodded. This was the signal for the big muscular man to say, 'All right, Inspector. You can go.'

Alvarado stared at the man, but he said nothing, he went round, slid into the car, punched the starter and drove off, heading in the direction of the coast highway. Only when he was well along, did he speak aloud a wondering curse. When *he'd* been a rookie detective *he* hadn't been that zealous, that thoroughly dedicated, and he couldn't remember any of the other rookies being that way either.

Maybe it was irritating, but it certainly had its beneficial side; if a homicide inspector couldn't get inside Elisabeth Fraser's house without being practically roughed up and searched, then obviously, no stranger was going to be able to make it either, regardless of how plausible his excuse for getting inside was, and *that* was comforting.

He ducked under the Santa Monica underpass, reached the highway that hugged the beaches of the Pacific Ocean, and boosted his vehicle to the maximum speed limit, and held it there. The alternative-route, which was inland, would have been quicker, but from Beverly Hills it was easier to head for the coast highway. He did not have a schedule, in any case, and regardless of how fast he drove or how much time he managed to save, he still was not going to be able to reach Lompoc, do what he had to do up there, and head for home, before evening, long after quitting time, so there was really not much point in trying to set any records.

This happened to be the time of year when holidayers, mostly from the Inner City, were streaking it for the open areas of the state, therefore most of the traffic was also travelling northward. Not that he was inconvenienced at all; regardless of how much traffic was pouring out of the city, the coast carriageway was more than ample to accommodate all of it.

He got hungry shortly before he reached the area where great, round, tan-dry hills came down to the very shoreline, which was in the vicinity of the turn-off he was looking for. He ate at a very nice seafood restaurant, listened to the conversation of a couple of fishermen who had not lucked-out, and with their heartfelt profanity still in his ears, he left the carriageway travelling inland, up through all that dry, hot, rolling country-side which seemed to very effectively block all the sea breezes before he'd travelled more than five miles.

But none of this was novel, he had come up to this area for rabbit hunting year in and year out, as a youngster. The only thing that *was* novel, when he finally came round the great, fat haunch of a fat hill and saw the village of Lompoc, was that the village he had not visited in something like fifteen years, was no longer just a village. It was now a town, and there were enough expensive residences, built as secluded retreats, as he cruised towards the town itself, to make what had once been a rustic, rural village drowsing away the decades in wonderful tree-shade, appear as an environ of Los Angeles, which, he thought as he drove along, was a tragedy.

10

A Productive Interlude

There were a lot of white walls, Moorish, curved doorways, and red tile roofs. Affluence had reached Lompoc since the days many years earlier when George Alvarado had come up to this summer-parched, rolling countryside with his friends, his cousins, and his parents. He did not remember the people they visited in Lompoc, except that they were relatives, distant ones, but the way it was, in the oldtime *Californio* families, kinship was a deep and abiding thing. As he cruised through town he felt a twinge of nostalgia, as much, actually, for his early youth, as for the people he had known in those days, and of whom he had heard practically nothing in the past ten years, since his parents had died. Different eras, different mores.

He paused beyond town scanning the

manzanita slopes which arose well beyond some sidehill vinyards. Since his boyhood, the natural groundcover had been pushed far beyond the edge of the village, and although, as he suspected, it was not feasible to make a living in this area as an agriculturist, that did not stop hundreds of people who made their wealth elsewhere, most notably in Los Angeles, from coming this far into the countryside to spend it, trying to create something agricultural.

But the skyline hadn't changed, and in all probability no matter how the state's population grew, the distant skylines probably would never change. For one thing, they were far too distant, too rugged, for people to want to colonise them, but the real reason would be simply because there was no water anywhere near their rims. Money was a great panacea, but it couldn't work marvels — miracles, perhaps, but not marvels.

He drove west, beyond the town, staying along the upland slopes and low hilltops as much as he could, studying the skyline, until he eventually found the somewhat saw-toothed skyline which had been used in the Shippen portraits.

Then he consulted his watch to estimate how much time he had before dusk closed down. Satisfied, he then concentrated upon the closer flow of land, the lifts and gentle drops, the swales, some farmed, some cultivated grassy pastures, seeking the exact spot where Leslie Shippen had set up his easel, and this was much more difficult and time-consuming. The skyline was distant, but it was also amenable to a long-spending sweeping vision. Closer down, the land spread out more, stretching picturesquely for many miles. The farther he drove, the more varied it became, until each half-mile, each quarter-mile, assumed a detailed and distinct differentness.

But he knew the spot was there, somewhere. All he had to do was keep the photographs upon the seat beside him, and continue searching. The natural landform was not changed, he was convinced of that. What he had to do was drive along until he had that notched skyline in direct perspective, then he would be either at the exact spot where Shippen had done his painting, or very close to it.

The light was different. Shippen had done his portrait and his landscape earlier in the day, perhaps about noon, or slightly after noon. Now, it was well into the afternoon, so the slanting sunrays made golden-hazy shadows in the distances. Alvarado paused upon one low hill, where the road ambled up and over, to contemplate a charmingly pastoral scene, and to tell himself that if he were a painter, this would be the time of day he would prefer.

Then he noticed something that had escaped his earlier attention. He was being followed by a man in a dark car. When he slowed, so did the other car, when he halted, the dark car eased down into the first available swale, and also halted.

The surprise diverted him from his search for a while. He tested his suspicion by driving down off a low knoll, then stopping out of sight in the ensuing swale, getting out of the car and walking over where several black-oaks stood, casting pleasant shade in dark patches all around.

The oncoming car crept to the low hilltop, halted, then eased forward until its driver could see down into the swale without the driver having to alight. The car then gently reversed, eased back far enough to be invisible down in the swale, and a large, lanky man climbed out and, keeping to the far side of his vehicle where Alvarado could not catch a good sighting of him, the lanky stranger slipped down the far side of the knoll, bearing towards the swale where Alvarado's car stood empty, in such a way that he could keep out of sight until he was close enough to walk directly up to Alvarado's car.

It was not a very long wait, and Alvarado was perfectly comfortable in the black-oak shade. He unbuttoned his jacket, leaned upon one of the trees, and patiently waited until the lanky man abruptly appeared, then dropped from sight and re-appeared much closer, and almost directly behind Alvarado's car.

Obviously, the lanky man's intention was to get up to the car while keeping the car's body between himself and the car's interior. As Alvarado watched, he smiled a little. Whoever he was, the lanky man put Alvarado in mind of an oldtime redskin warrior creeping up on a wagon.

Then the stranger came erect and began walking swiftly forward. That was when Alvarado saw the gun in his hand, and the glint of red sunlight off the badge on his shirt.

Alvarado waited, allowing the deputy sheriff plenty of time to verify that the Los Angeles Police Department was the registered owner of his car, then he ambled forth from the shade, and while the deputy was leaning in on the driver's side examining the registration slip on the steering-column, Alvarado said, 'Good afternoon, Deputy,' and kept on ambling along as the lanky man jerked back and whirled, erect and ready.

Alvarado dug out his ID folder and smiled as he crossed the last fifty feet. 'I couldn't get a good view of your car when

I decided I was being followed, so I took evasive action.'

The deputy put up his weapon, examined Alvarado's identification, handed back the folder and thumbed back his hat as he said, 'That's a relief, Inspector. I thought I had one.'

'One what?'

'This time of summer we always get hippie-types up through the county; they'll steal anything that isn't chained down. Some folks back a mile or so saw you cruising along, looking the country over, and called in.' The deputy, who was in his mid twenties, had a nice smile. 'Mind telling me what you're looking for?'

Alvarado said, 'No,' and reached into his car for the picture of the three men. 'I'm looking for the exact spot where this was painted.'

The deputy looked, then his smile broadened. 'Well hell, that's no problem. Mind telling me *why* you want to find this spot?'

'I want to see if someone around there, saw the man who made this painting, and those three men in the picture, who were up here with him.'

The deputy nodded, studying Alvarado thoughtfully. 'Someone broke a law, maybe, Inspector?'

Alvarado took back the picture and tossed it into the car as he answered. 'Yeah. Someone broke the law, Deputy. Someone murdered all four of those men. The Mexicans first, then the guy who painted the pictures.'

The deputy sheriff blinked. In a place like Lompoc crime was never rampant, and murders, when they were committed, were ordinarily very basic; someone shot his wife's lover, or hit a pedestrian while drunk-driving, but even then, there was only one victim per crime, so the deputy sheriff's stare was both excusable and understandable.

'All *four*, Inspector?'

'Yeah. Now, about the place where . . . '

'It's down the road a piece. Maybe three, four miles. I can take you out there. But maybe I ought to tell you first that I talked to those fellers. This happened about a year back, and it happened about the same way as I got the call about you. Someone called our office saying four men were up to something out on the game preserve, so I went out there. The man who was doing the art work was named . . . '

'Leslie Shippen?'

'Yeah, that was it. Leslie Shippen. I should have remembered that, because Lesley also happens to be my wife's first name. I guess it's one of those names, like Francis, folks hang on their kids without it making much difference whether it's a boy or a girl. Anyway, I talked to this Shippen-character for about a half hour, looked over all his identification, then talked to the pepper-bellies. There wasn't anything wrong with what they were doing, and the guy really was an artist. While I was standing around, he posed those other three guys, and sketched them first. He was one hell of a handy artist, I can tell you that, Inspector.' The deputy paused for breath, or to emphasise his statement concerning Leslie Shippen. Then he said, 'There was another guy came cruising along while I was out there.

He was from Los Angeles, too. He was going up to the lake for some bass fishing, but he stopped when he saw the sheriff's car, thinking someone might have been hurt or something. I remember his name; it was Henry Fielding.'

Alvarado's interest switched abruptly from the place where Shippen had done his portrait to the man named Henry Fielding. 'This fisherman,' he said, 'how do you know he was from Los Angeles?'

'Said so, when he walked over and introduced himself.'

'Did he stay long?'

The deputy's answer was a disappointment. 'Can't say, Inspector. I pulled out shortly after he came along. There wasn't much point in me hanging around, Shippen and the three Messicans were legitimate, and anyway, I got a call to come on back in, over the intercom, so I headed back for town.'

'Do you remember anything else about Fielding?' Alvarado asked, hopefully.

The lanky deputy rubbed his jaw. 'Well; it was a new Cadillac, pretty elegant car to go fishing in, but then, rich people from Los Angeles do a lot of funny things. I think the licence number began with three letters in sequence . . . DEF, that was it. I remember that because it's sort of phonetic, like deaf. I don't remember the number though. Didn't have any reason to.'

'Anything else? Was Fielding tall, short, dark, light . . . ?'

'Average in build and size, Inspector, a little thin on top, maybe fifty, fifty-five years of age, fair complected.'

'Would you recognise him again?'

The deputy nodded. 'Yeah. I don't forget people — only names, and I usually write them down, if I think I might want to know them later. But this guy was just . . . ' The deputy's gaze narrowed. 'You're interested in Fielding, too?'

Alvarado was candid with the lanky man. 'I don't have a damned thing on the murderer. Except that the press calls him the fire ant. They picked that up from the *Chicano* newspapers down in L.A.'

'I read something about him a few weeks back in a Los Angeles newspaper. I wondered at the time where the hell they got a name like that,' the deputy said.

Alvarado didn't explain. 'Fielding, if that's his name, was probably a contact for Shippen; he may even have come up here to a rendezvous with all four of them, Shippen and the three *Chicanos*. That's my theory right at this moment. Maybe I'm all wrong, but this is the first contact I've been able to come up with. When I get back to L.A. I'm going to see what I can turn up on Fielding. If there's a picture, I'll send it up to you for identification.'

The deputy said, 'You do that. Like I told you, I don't forget faces, only names. I'll recognise the guy, all right.'

Alvarado smiled. 'I'm obliged. Mind telling me your name?'

'Homer Wetzel.' The deputy pumped Alvarado's hand, and watched as Alvarado got into his car. 'I hope you get this guy,' he said, as Alvarado punched the starter. 'This fire ant feller.'

Alvarado backed clear, turned around, and headed back in the direction of Lompoc. Mid-way along, he poked his head out and scanned the reddening lateday sky. He hadn't expected to get back to Los Angeles until night, in any case, and he still did not expect to, nor would he be able to, but even so, he would get back an hour or two earlier than he had expected.

By the time he reached the coast freeway again, and went in search of a pay-phone to call Captain Murphy, as he'd been requested to do, it was almost fully dark.

After making the telephone call, he took his time about driving back. He had something fresh to ponder, and he also had all the time he'd need to do that.

11

An Elusive Burglar

Turning up a name like Henry Fielding was not very productive, except in the literal sense; there were a dozen 'Henry Fieldings' listed in the city telephone book, and probably, if Alvarado had got very diligent about it, and rummaged through the city directory as well as the directories of the outlying communities, he could have turned up another half dozen or more. But he hadn't expected to be very lucky, anyway, so there was no sense of disappointment.

He called Sacramento for a 'make' on a late model Cadillac car with the letters DEF as the prefix for the licence number, and while he was cognizant of the custom the Department of Motor Vehicles had of issuing licences on an annual basis, in sequences, to particular areas, which would mean that if the prefix DEF were issued in the Los Angeles area, there would undoubtedly be several thousand cars with that prefix to their licence numbers, he was also confident that when this was narrowed down to *Cadillacs* bearing that prefix, the number would be drastically reduced. And he was right. By the time DMV called back, shortly before noon, Alvarado was informed that sixty-six late model Cadillacs had DEF prefixes, and DMV was teletyping that list down to LAPD right away.

Alvarado went out to lunch, took his time, and as he returned, later, and went along to Communications to pick up the DMV list, it was on hand.

He ambled back upstairs studying the list, and nearly collided with Captain Murphy in the upstairs corridor near the lifts.

Murphy turned and went back to the office with Alvarado, his interest piqued by that telephone call the previous night.

They discussed Alvarado's talk with the deputy sheriff on the outskirts of Lompoc, and Alvarado showed Captain Murphy his list of cars. Murphy, who made a practice of resisting pressure from the Commissioner's office, the newspapers, alarmed citizens, groups which clamoured for immediate arrests after every major crime, looked relieved when Alvarado said he thought they were finally moving in the right direction. Murphy still looked relieved when he departed fifteen minutes later, leaving Alvarado to begin his struggle to find the Cadillac with the prefix DEF, which belonged to someone who had been out of the city, ostensibly on a fishing trip, about a year earlier.

None of the names of registered owners on the DMV list even sounded like Henry Fielding. Alvarado had a number of alternatives to facilitate his manhunt, but every one of them entailed a tedious, name-by-name search, and locating someone who didn't have an alibi for a particular day a year earlier, wasn't even a good option for someone who had a year to make that kind of search in.

Sixty-six names was not a great number, unless they had to be researched individually, then they became something else.

Alvarado took his list down to Records and Files in an effort to establish that at least one of those names had a police record, but even that was nothing which could be accomplished in a short space of time, computers notwithstanding, because, once a felony record was disclosed, the name had to be matched to a late model Cadillac, with the DEF prefix.

But it could be done before quitting time. Alvarado got that assurance from the attractive, willowy female clerk who took the list from him, so he promised to call back by five o'clock, and headed back for his office.

He hadn't been at his desk ten minutes before he received a telephone call from Albert Knowland. Expecting an impatient quiz concerning the voluntary house-arrest of Knowland's daughter, Alvarado leaned back braced for an argument, and Knowland caught him completely off-guard with his first sentence.

'Someone tried to get into Shippen's

apartment last night. I went out back to the car port to drive over and take some things to Elisabeth, and saw a light up there, through the window of the upstairs landing. I went back to my apartment to call the police, and a man came past my front window walking very fast, so I went outside. He ran down the street, got into a car and drove off.'

Alvarado's first impulse was to ask for a description. Instead, he said, 'What kind of a car?'

Knowland was uncertain. 'Dark, I think. He had parked beneath some old trees, and it was about ten o'clock at night, so that's about all I could be sure of.'

'A compact,' asked Alvarado, 'A medium-sized car, or a large car?'

'Large. It wasn't a compact, I'm sure of that.'

'Large, dark and shiny?'

'Yes, it was dark and shiny, I'm quite sure, and now that I think about it, it was a large car.'

Alvarado sighed. 'All right. Did you call the police?'

'Well, no,' replied Elisabeth Fraser's

father. 'When I was sure he had gone, I went upstairs, and I'm sure he'd been trying to force the door, there were marks on the casings.'

Alvarado was already arising when he said, 'I'll be along in a few minutes,' and replaced the telephone.

On his way out to the car it occurred to Alvarado that if the fire ant-killer had been the person at the studio apartment, he had probably gone there to remove something, and the first thing that popped into Alvarado's mind was that portrait of Holquin, Gomez and Mendez — which Captain Murphy had told Alvarado to impound several days ago, and which Alvarado had done nothing about.

But there had to be more to it than that. If the fire ant was only now seeking the incriminating portrait, when he certainly had known it existed even before he killed Leslie Shippen, then he must have very recently discovered something else — that the police were perhaps aware of a connection between the fire ant's first three victims, and his most recent victim, Leslie Shippen.

As Alvarado drove to Palm Drive, he had a very unpleasant thought: Yesterday, he had talked to a deputy sheriff up near Lompoc about a possible connection, not just between Shippen, the three *Chicanos*, but also possibly between a fourth man, Henry Fielding, and today, or at least last night, perhaps four or five hours *after* his conversation with the deputy sheriff, the fire ant made a desperate attempt to steal the incriminating portrait.

He hoped very hard it was a coincidence. If it wasn't, then a deputy sheriff named Homer Wetzel had to have contacted the fire ant. At least this was an unavoidable possibility. George Alvarado had not spoken to anyone else at great length about his suspicions, except to Captain Murphy, and that had only been this morning.

When he alighted out front of the apartment building, Albert Knowland was waiting, on the patio. He nodded to Alvarado, and turned abruptly to lead the way upstairs to the doorway of the

Shippen residence.

The marks were there, on the wood-work, exactly as Albert Knowland had said they were, but Alvarado's practised eyes detected more than just pry-bar marks, so he unlocked the door, entered the stale-smelling apartment, and with Elisabeth Fraser's father on his heels, went directly to the bedroom, to the closet where the paintings were kept, and without a word began to very systematically place the paintings along the wall.

The portrait of Holquin, Mendez and Gomez, was missing.

He went back over the paintings a second time, searched the closet from the shelves downward, and into each corner. The portrait was not there.

Finally, he went through the other rooms, foot by foot, not expecting to turn up the portrait because he knew exactly where he had left it — in the closet with the other paintings — and of course, it was nowhere in the apartment. Finally, still with Albert Knowland dogging his footsteps, Alvarado called in for a lab team to come out and go over the apartment for fingerprints, anything at all they might find which could establish anything at all about the burglar.

Not that he was at all hopeful, but this was a routine procedure.

While he was standing beside the carved desk, he remembered the pair of daggers and the loaded automatic with the pearl handles, and opened several drawers to verify that they were still there. This time, though, he appropriated them all. He was turning, when something in the back of his mind registered a void. Very slowly he turned back, scanning the room as he moved his head. There was another painting missing; the one Leslie Shippen had done of Elisabeth Fraser. Shippen's nude, his last oil portrait.

The stand was still there. Even the discarded palette and the small containers with solvent in them for Shippen's brushes, were still there. Just the portrait was gone.

Knowland noticed this, when he saw where the detective was staring. For a moment the older man simply stared, then he gave a slight start and burst into speech.

'My gawd; he took the one of Elisabeth too. Inspector; he *knows*. He's got to know she's helping the police. Otherwise, why would he take her portrait?'

Knowland's anxious tone annoyed Alvarado. He strolled closer for a look at the solvent-containers and the easel before answering.

'What does he know, Mr. Knowland? What *can* he know? It was a beautiful portrait. Anyone would have wanted to own it. He was here, had got the painting he came after, and for all I know, he admires good art, and took the painting of your daughter for that reason.' Alvarado turned towards the agitated older man. 'Except between you and your daughter, my superior and me, who knows your daughter has even spoken to the police?'

Albert Knowland said nothing, but his worry seemed to lessen a little, not entirely, but a little, as he said, 'I don't like it, Inspector. It scares the hell out of me. This man has already killed four people. I tried to keep Elisabeth from getting involved at all, and if anything happens to her — it's your fault. You remember that, it'll be your fault.'

Alvarado herded Knowland out of the apartment, locked the door, and herded Knowland all the way back to the patio without saying another word, but when they were down there, Alvarado's irritability had atrophied to the point where he could speak without sounding antagonistic.

'I'll have a man sent up here to stake out the apartment, Mr. Knowland. Not that it'll do any good, now that the fire ant has been here, but because it ought to make you rest easier at night. And one more thing; don't go up there. Stay completely away from Shippen's diggings.'

Knowland drew up very erect. 'Do I look stupid, Inspector? I wouldn't go near that apartment again for ten thousand dollars.'

Alvarado returned to his car, called in for a man to be stationed in the studio, ascertained that the laboratory team had already been dispatched, then drove slowly back to the same kosher delicatessen where he had lunched once before, and even had the same table, when he ate a belated midday meal.

He was calmer, now, and was inclined to believe the break-in, while perhaps not entirely coincidental, did not really involve Deputy Sheriff Homer Wetzel. But it certainly did suggest that the fire ant now knew the police were not letting up in their efforts to find him, to find whoever it was who had killed Leslie Shippen, and, if the police had found that portrait, then they would also know the fire ant was the killer of Holquin, Mendez and Gomez.

He had, of course, performed his burglary two days too late. Captain Murphy would be annoyed over Alvarado not bringing in the portrait, as Murphy had instructed him to do, but the portrait had been photographed, and that was the next best thing to having the original picture.

How, Alvarado wondered, did the fire ant happen to go after that painting? Had he only just recalled that Shippen had made the portrait, up near Lompoc, a year earlier? That did not seem altogether plausible, but until Alvarado knew more about the fire ant, himself, as an individual human being, he was not going to be able to determine whether the killer actually knew the police were getting closer to him, whether he might have an inside source to confirm this, or whether the fire ant had just, coincidentally, burglarised Shippen's apartment.

If the fire ant knew Alvarado had been up to Lompoc the previous day, and had established the fact that Shippen, Holquin, Mendez and Gomez, had met a man up there calling himself Henry Fielding, then the fire ant could very simply deduce the rest of it — which was, simply, that the police were indeed, getting very close to him.

12

The Mills Grind Slowly —
But They Grind

Captain Murphy accepted Alvarado's report philosophically for the best of all reasons; there was not a damned thing he could do to reverse what had happened.

He did not even sarcastically remind Alvarado of his admonition about bringing in the portrait. All he said was, 'If that son of a bitch doesn't leave the city, and probably also the country, he's not very bright.'

Later, Alvarado took the pearl-handled automatic pistol and the pair of daggers down to the laboratory for routine examination, identification, and, if possible in the case of the daggers, some sort of authenticated history. He was not hopeful, and he was not very interested, either.

Files and Records had the completed

list of Cadillac-owners with licence numbers beginning with DEF, shown to have police records.

It was an interesting compilation of people who drove new Cadillac cars in an era of petrol shortages, when most other Americans were trying to conserve, but then, as Alvarado philosophised as he read the names, and the crimes those people had been taken into custody for presumably committing, people devoid of ethics and morality wouldn't consider themselves involved in anything alien to their personal cults of individualism, anyway.

He had no difficulty in weeding out nineteen woman Cadillac-owners. Nor did he have any trouble eliminating nine negroes, and that helped whittle down the list a bit. There were eleven practising physicians, whose names he wrote separately for investigation only if he couldn't turn up better suspects, and the best possibility of all, a man named Al Scarpinato, notorious throughout the entire State of California as a hoodlum, had died only the week before, and

Alvarado had read of his demise, at the time, with professional pleasure, but now, coming across that man's name, he regretted the passing.

He capsuled the remaining names, called the DMV up in Sacramento for photographs from the copies of each individual driver's permit, then left the building, got into his car and drove out to Sorrel Lane, to the charming Spanish-style residence of Elisabeth Fraser.

This time, he was passed through the protective screening by a swarthy detective named Bastinado, whose nick-name was known to Alvarado, although he had never used it, and while he stood briefly chatting with Bastinado, it occurred to him that it might not be a good idea to call Bastinado by his nickname, even when they were both smiling; Bastinado was the bare minimum for a Los Angeles policeman, five feet and nine inches in height, but he was certainly otherwise well within the requirements; he was built like a Sherman tank, and was hard as iron, and probably weighed two hundred pounds, all of it bone and muscle.

Bastinado also knew Alvarado. He called him '*Gachupín*,' then grinned from ear to ear. But Alvarado did not use Bastinado's nickname — *el bastardo* — he simply said, 'You'll think I'm wearing spurs, if anyone gets to the lady in this house, while you're on duty, *peon*.'

Bastinado's good-natured broad smile lingered. 'President Ford couldn't get in that house, *Gachupín*.' Bastinado considered that a moment, then changed it a little. '*Especially* President Ford.'

'Anyone tried to get in?' asked Alvarado.

Bastinado shook his head. 'Her father. Otherwise no one's been around. Tell me something, Inspector: What's new on the fire ant?'

Alvarado replied with an impassive expression. 'Nothing. And you know damned well that if I had him in hip pocket, I wouldn't tell you.'

Bastinado sighed. 'You wait. Give me five years, until I get up there where you are, in Homicide. I'll show you how to catch guys like that.'

Alvarado considered the massively

powerful, squatty man in front of him. 'Within five years you're going to be so damned fat they'll have to put overload springs on a car for you.' He walked towards the patio with the swarthy man glowering after him.

Elisabeth Fraser admitted him to the house. There were lights on in the sitting room, small, amber-coloured side-wall candelabra-type electrical fixtures. The light they gave off, and the fixtures themselves, were perfectly in keeping with the décor. Alvarado looked around, then said, 'You know, this is how Hollywood believes the oldtime native Californians lived.'

She said, 'Didn't they?'

'No. They didn't even have glass windows. They used to scrape rawhide until it was paper thin. That's what they used in place of glass. It let light in, and kept bugs out.' He strolled to a chair. 'My grandmother told me that. And all the furniture they had, they made themselves, and it wasn't very good, nor very extensive.'

She stood looking over where he was

sitting. 'Those were your forefathers, then, Inspector Alvarado?'

'Yeah. They owned thousands of acres right where the city is now, and they barely made it from year to year. If beans and peppers hadn't been good dryland crops, they wouldn't have eaten anything but stringy beef.'

'But they had freedom, and space,' she said, moving towards the sofa.

He thought about that for a moment, then conceded it. 'Yes. And they were very close, in their family life. I suppose it was a good way to live.' He smiled at her. 'At least they didn't have much crime. Do you know why? Because they had so darn little worth stealing.'

She laughed with him. 'And you, Inspector?'

He wasn't quite sure what she meant by that, so he shrugged. 'Me, I'm a product of the *gringo* world. I didn't even have the decency to be born with brown eyes, a great disappointment to my father.' He gazed across the amber-lighted room at her. 'And you, Mrs. Fraser?'

'My people came from Missouri, but I

was born here, which makes me a native — although I don't have brown eyes either.'

'Your eyes are grey-green, and they are beautiful,' he said, then cleared his throat and sat forward on the chair. 'Do you know anyone named Henry Fielding?'

She turned the name over in her mind before replying. 'No, I don't think so. If I ever met him, I don't remember it.'

'Not by that name,' he murmured. 'An older man, possibly in his fifties, balding, average height and build, who happens to drive a new Cadillac, which is dark coloured. Does that ring any bells?'

It didn't. 'No. I'm sorry. Who is he?'

'You're not supposed to ask, and I'm not supposed to tell you.'

Her eyes crinkled in faint, wry humour. 'All right. Then forget I asked. Otherwise, how is the investigation coming along?'

'Someone broke into Shippen's studio and stole that nude of you, and the portrait of those three *Chicanos* I showed you the photograph of.'

She was not upset. 'I know. My father called me early this morning. He was upset. I think you'd already been there, but he didn't mention that.'

'Then how did you know I'd been there?'

She looked coolly at him. 'How else could he have got inside Leslie's apartment? If you've figured him out as well as I imagine you have, then you know he wouldn't go in there unless a policeman was with him.'

Alvarado pondered this a moment, before saying, 'You are an unusual woman, Mrs. Fraser.'

She laughed a little self-consciously. 'Not really; after all, I've known him all my life. But getting back to the portraits . . . am I allowed to ask about them?'

'You can ask, but I can't tell you anything because I honestly don't know anything more than I've already told you — someone stole them.'

The green eyes remained fixed on his face. 'Mr. Fielding, then . . . ?'

Alvarado shifted position in the chair before speaking. 'You really *are* unusual. Was that question based upon a deduction?'

'Yes; that's the only thing you've said since walking into the house, that was new to me. So, I logically assumed Mr. Fielding might have had something to do with the burglary.' She smiled at Alvarado's steady stare in her direction. 'Inspector, have you had dinner?'

He hadn't, but he wasn't going to have it in her house, even though he was not technically on duty. 'I had a late lunch,' he said, stretching the truth a bit in order to sidle out from under the impending invitation. Then he used diversion to get her mind off dinner. 'You seem to be bearing up well under this confinement.'

She made a small hand-gesture. 'If I have to do something, Inspector, then I simply do it. Anyway, I have great faith in the police. This won't last much longer. You'll find the murderer soon.' She smiled again. 'A highball, then, if not dinner?'

He declined that too. 'No thank you.'

'Fraternising is *verboten*, then?'

'Something like that, Mrs. Fraser,' he said, and arose to stride across and stand about ten feet from the portrait of her partial profile on the front wall. 'You told me you'd never been up in the Lompoc area, didn't you?'

She hesitated briefly before replying, 'Yes, I told you that . . . Inspector, do you doubt it?'

He turned, facing her. 'I certainly don't *want* to doubt it.'

'But you do?'

He clasped both hands behind his back. 'No; not definitely. But something happened last night and yesterday that makes me wonder if the man who broke into Shippen's studio and stole those pictures, didn't know I was going up to Lompoc yesterday, and aside from a deputy sheriff up there, you were the only other person, aside from my immediate superior, who knew I was going up there.' He waited for a reaction, but there was none. Her face remained slightly puzzled, slightly irritated.

She said, 'How could I have told anyone?'

'By the telephone,' he replied, then strolled back to the chair and sank down again. 'I can have the outgoing calls traced by their numbers.'

She was angry, finally, 'Please do, Inspector. I spoke to my father twice, once in the morning and again about dinner-time last evening. Those were the only calls I made yesterday.'

He offered her his most disarming smile. 'I believe you.'

That left her hanging in mid-air. She still showed anger, but the look gradually died out. She finally said, 'I wish I knew whether I liked you or not,' then she arose.

Alvarado climbed back up out of the chair. He was being dismissed, which was acceptable to him, he hadn't really called to badger her, anyway. In fact, he hadn't had a valid reason at all, for stopping by, except that she was in his mind when he'd left his office.

When they were over by the door, she made another comment that intrigued him. 'Inspector, if the person who stole that portrait of those three men had only taken that particular picture, wouldn't it seem reasonable to assume that he thought you might have finally connected

Leslie Shippen with those three men?'

'Very reasonable,' he told her.

'But then he also took the other painting.'

Alvarado told her fundamentally the same thing he had said to her father. 'Maybe he appreciates fine art. Anyone would be pleased to have that portrait of you, Mrs. Fraser.'

'Unless, Inspector, he didn't want it for the sake of art. Unless he wanted it so that he could identify me by it?'

Alvarado sighed. He was going to have to go through that routine again, this time for the daughter. 'Mrs. Fraser, if you're thinking the fire ant got your picture — well — maybe he did. But he doesn't know you're here, under police protection. How would he know that?'

She stunned Alvarado with her quiet answer. 'Inspector — whoever he was, when he came into the apartment to kill Leslie, he most certainly *knew* Leslie Shippen, and granting that, then he certainly knew Leslie was an artist — and since Leslie had been working on that wet canvas of me over by the window, he would also know — perhaps not right then, but he'd have realised it later — that Leslie had been working from life; had been using a live model . . . He would have realised later that the live model had been in the apartment at the time he killed Leslie. I'm only glad he was too otherwise occupied during the killing to think of it, or I probably wouldn't be standing here with you right now, would I?'

Alvarado stood in silence with his hand on the door-knob for a long moment, then said, 'Goodnight, Mrs. Fraser,' and let himself out of the house.

13

A Sense Of Urgency

He had never doubted that Elisabeth Fraser was an intelligent individual, but being thoroughly masculine, he would have preferred to think of her in a different way. The difficulty arose now, as he drove to his flat, when he tried to reconcile the soft, beautifully alluring Elisabeth Fraser, with the woman who had stood at the door with him, calmly and rationally working out an exercise in logic, which he had quite overlooked.

By the time he had showered, had got his glass of beer and had gone into the sitting room to switch on the nightly newscast, he was thinking only of the logical Elisabeth Fraser.

If she was correct, if the fire ant had stolen her portrait in order to memorise her face so that he could perhaps hunt her down, because he thought she might have been a witness to his slaying of Leslie Shippen, then the fire ant was going to have one hell of a time of it, finding her, and if he managed, in time, to do that, he was going to find it even more difficult to reach her.

But Alvarado had respect for the fire ant, too. While he drank beer and listened to the steady flow of gloom and menace coming forth from the newscaster, he decided to double the guard on the Sorrel Lane residence.

Later, when he retired, he felt slightly uncomfortable about using Elisabeth Fraser as bait. He also recalled something Captain Murphy had said, about telling her she was being used like this.

In the morning, drinking his first cup of coffee for the day, it occurred to him that however this assignment ended, it was now entering its crucial phase. He was fairly certain he would have the fire ant's identity by evening, or, at the very latest, the next day. He was also just a little worried over the fire ant's ability to trace down Elisabeth Fraser. Regardless of what he had thought the previous evening, there was one clear fact worth pondering: The fire ant was a very resourceful individual.

By the time he reached the office and put in the call for an additional surveillance team to take positions in the vicinity of the Sorrel Lane residence, he was convinced that the tempo of the investigation was subtly gathering momentum.

A Department of Motor Vehicle employee came to the office shortly before ten o'clock in the morning with an envelope from the Sacramento office for Inspector George Alvarado. The employee had been up in Sacramento at a conference the previous day, had been handed the envelope to deliver, and had brought it with him on the flight south. Alvarado was pleased, and thanked the messenger warmly.

Inside, were a number of those small, face-forward, photographs which were mandatory in California, for every driver's permit. He sifted through them hopefully, saw none that meant anything to him, went up to Captain Murphy's

158

office with a request that made Murphy look momentarily blank, then launched into an explanation.

'The fire ant may believe that Elisabeth Fraser saw him kill Leslie Shippen. He may have stolen her portrait so that he could memorise her face, then hunt her down. Jerry, in this bunch of little photographs is the face of the fire ant. I'll bet a month's wages on that. There is only one person I know of who can identify the fire ant. He's that deputy sheriff I talked to up at Lompoc. The reason I want you to clear a leave of absence for him through the sheriff's office up there, then send one of our traffic helicopters up for him, and bring him down here, is so that he can pick out the face of the fire ant. All he's got to do is fly down here. I'll meet him at the airport. He can look at the photos, pick out the one I want, for me, then they can fly him back. It shouldn't take more than about three hours, altogether. The sheriff up there ought to co-operate that much. Once Deputy Wetzel fingers the fire ant, I'll go get him. While you're clearing

Wetzel for the flight down, and talking Traffic into letting us use one of their choppers for a couple of hours, I'll go get a John Doe warrant for arrest from the clerk of the court.'

Captain Murphy squirmed. 'Why in the hell can't you just drive back up there and let this deputy sheriff . . . ?'

'Because, Jerry, the fire ant isn't going to sit on his hands.'

'Oh hell,' growled the captain of detectives, 'he can't get to her, even if he can find out where she is.'

Alvarado said, 'You want to bet on it? I can think of four damned good reasons why we can't take that chance. The four reasons were named Shippen, Holquin, Mendez and . . . '

'All right.' Captain Murphy scowled at the telephone atop his desk. 'They don't like to loan their helicopters, and you know it.'

'Jerry . . . '

'I said all right! Go get your warrant and come back here.'

Alvarado left the office, walking fast. He felt no particular satisfaction, just a sense of relief, and urgency. Getting the John Doe warrant was not a problem, particularly for Homicide Division, although the courts did not favour this kind of an arrest warrant because it implied that Homicide did not have an actual identification, and arresting people as 'John Doe' left the city wide open to false-arrest lawsuits.

If the particulars were valid, though, the warrant would be issued. In Alvarado's case, there was no trouble; all he got from the consenting justice, and the vinegary court-clerk who did the paperwork, was a cold look and, from His Honour, a tart comment.

'If it was almost anyone else, you wouldn't get it, and even with you, Alvarado, I'm not enthusiastic. You've never got us into hot water, but sooner or later you will, if you keep this up.'

Alvarado took the rebuke, and the chilly looks meekly. Eating a small portion of crow was worth it.

When he returned to Captain Murphy's office the captain was out but his secretary had all the details. Traffic had consented and the helicopter was now on its way up-country. The sheriff had given his consent, and Deputy Wetzel would be at the Lompoc airport awaiting the helicopter's arrival.

So far, it had all gone smoothly. Alvarado consulted his wristwatch, then left the building with the packet of photographs, went across to the cafe where he usually ate, when he was at his office, and spent a half hour over a cup of coffee, with those little photographs spread out on the table.

He could, of course, have gone back to File and Records to make comparisons of the photographs from DMV with the LAPD pictures, and he could also have brought along all the data on the people he was interested in, but all he wanted at the moment was an identification. Once that had been taken care of, he'd delve into the rest of it.

Captain Murphy came in, looked around, saw Alvarado, and crossed to the table. As he pulled out a chair, and saw all the small photographs, he said, 'Suppose he's not there?' and sat down to gesture for coffee to a nearby waitress.

Alvarado had no doubts. 'He's there, don't worry about that.'

After the coffee arrived Alvarado began putting the pictures back in their envelope. 'Thanks for getting things lined up,' he said, and smiled across the table.

Captain Murphy shrugged, sipped coffee, glanced around, then blew out a big breath. 'I'm tired and it's not even midday yet.' He fixed small, bright eyes on Alvarado. 'If you get this guy by tomorrow night, you'll still be able to go on holiday on schedule. How's that for an inducement?'

Alvarado hadn't thought about his vacation in over a week. 'If I get him by tomorrow night I'll be willing to go on a vacation. I wonder if she knows how to fish?'

'What?'

'Nothing.' Alvarado tucked the envelope into a jacket pocket and glanced at his wrist. 'How long did the chopper pilot think it'd take him to get up there, and back down here?'

Murphy drained his coffee cup before

replying. 'I didn't talk to the pilot, only to the department head, then to a dispatcher. They thought it might take about three hours, like we figured. If there aren't any screwups, and there'd better not be, I had practically to promise half my pension to those Scrooges. Well; in a way I don't blame them. It's hard enough to do your job with a full complement, and nobody knows that better than I do, without having other departments wanting to borrow from you.'

Alvarado had plenty of time, but he was restless. As he arose, Murphy said, 'Speaking of doing my job without a full complement — what the hell did you send two more vigilantes out to Sorrel Lane for? There are going to be cops stumbling over cops out there.'

Alvarado grinned. 'Be patient, Captain. One more day and you can put everyone back on the treadmill. You said it yourself . . . I got to worrying about the fire ant's ability to find her.'

Murphy must have already guessed as much. 'Nobody's going to get into the house, put your mind to rest about that.'

Alvarado nodded and departed. It was a considerable drive to the municipal airport, even without midday traffic to make it worse, but he still had plenty of time.

The day was hot, the humidity was high, the heat was uncomfortably muggy, and this was only morning. By mid-afternoon it was going to be a fiercely unpleasant day.

It did not matter that this was springtime, not in Southern California where summer was eight or nine months long, and winter was only different from summer when it rained, or when frost came in the night, and otherwise the days were commonly warm-to-hot.

Alvarado was accustomed to the heat; he didn't mind it. He'd grown up with it, actually did not know much about other climates, but Southern California's weather had been steadily changing for the past quarter century, until the heat, thoroughly impregnated with foul air, onion-scented, greyish smog, made breathing almost poisonous. This, he had never become accustomed to. Like all other Angelenos, he complained about the eye-stinging smog, but that's as far as it seemed to go. A few half-hearted attempts at cleaning the atmosphere had been undertaken, from time to time, but industrial chimneys and millions of cars spewing clouds of exhaust fumes still prevailed. Cleaning an atmosphere, it seemed, was only successful when it was not something that collided with an economy based upon polluting an atmosphere. Aesthetics never fared very well, when they competed with money.

By the time Alvarado reached the airport, he was in a part of the city where industrial air pollution so completely clogged the atmosphere that landing lights burned all day as well as all night, and where people actually wore gauze masks to protect their respiratory equipment.

He left his car, entered the huge, stadium-sized waiting room, looked for, and found, the Airport Security Office, went in there, and was relieved by the filter-variety of an air-conditioner that not only kept the office cool, but also supplied it with clean air.

He was taken by an attractive secretary to the desk of a grizzled, greying, thickly-made older man. When he showed his ID folder, explained his purpose in being at the airport, the grizzled man leaned back and pointed out a large window.

'See those red and white pylons, Inspector? That's where all police aircraft land. That's their private area. Your chopper will be directed to that area when he calls in for clearance to land.'

The grizzled man fixed Alvarado with testy blue eyes, and picked up some papers from atop his desk. 'Anything else?'

Alvarado got out of there, wondering if working in a place where the air was deadly, where the constant noise and congestion were compounded hourly, made people surly and un-smiling. He decided that it had to be like that, found his way out of the barn-like building, strolled to the restricted area, and found a patch of shade with a stone bench conveniently close by, then sat down to wait.

According to his watch he had roughly an hour to kill. Providing everything had gone off properly up at Lompoc. He hoped that it had, not just because he did not like the idea of sitting around this busy, clamouring, evil-smelling place any longer than he had to, but also because of what Captain Murphy had said about having practically to beg to get the helicopter, and having to make concessions to-boot.

Jumbo jets arrived and took off with a great din, and trailing slip-streams of black exhaust fumes. Airplanes of every variety flew in, or flew out, or were stranded on the ground in every direction as far as Alvarado could see. People, like ants, swarmed everywhere. Alvarado sat and watched, and felt dwarfed to ant-size.

14

An Identification, Finally

Deputy Sheriff Homer Wetzel did not look especially out of place, in his khaki uniform and wearing his regulation, embossed black leather belt and holstered weapon, but evidently he felt out of place, because the first thing he said when he shook hands with George Alvarado, was: 'This sure is a busy, noisy, bad-smelling place.'

The helicopter pilot remained out with his vehicle. When Alvarado asked how the flight had been, Deputy Wetzel was more nonchalant. 'About average. I flew in one of those things about every couple of weeks on my tour of duty in Viet-Nam.'

Alvarado took the deputy inside, to the coffee shop, where they got a table in a corner. As he drew out the DMV envelope Alvarado made certain that Deputy Wetzel knew why he had been brought down to Los Angeles. Wetzel knew. 'Your captain made it pretty plain to the sheriff. You got the pictures?'

Alvarado wordlessly emptied the envelope, then began arranging the little photographs so that they were aligned, facing Wetzel. The deputy glanced at them, and said, 'Department of Motor Vehicles give you these?'

Alvarado conceded that, then leaned as a waitress appeared, asked for two coffees, and did not allow Deputy Wetzel even to glance up as he pushed several of the photographs closer, across the table.

Wetzel's examination was quick and incisive. He had not impressed Alvarado as being a fast-thinking man; he certainly did not move nor speak rapidly. But after only a few moments of studying all those little pictures, he unerringly reached, picked out a particular photo, and flipped it over in front of Alvarado.

'That's your man, Inspector.'

Alvarado looked, then raised his eyes. 'Are you sure?'

'Yeah, I'm sure.'

'You'll probably be subpoenaed to

testify, if I pick this guy up.'

Wetzel still did not hesitate. 'It won't be the first time. I've testified in my share of cases. And that's the man I saw up there, last year, talking to Shippen and those three beaners.'

Alvarado turned the photograph over. The name on the reverse side was Donald Philip Robinson. There were several DMV symbols, and some numbers under the name, then the date the photograph had been taken, which was three years earlier.

Wetzel, leaning to look closer, said, 'Those damned symbols are for his residential area. Any DMV office can break them down for you.' Wetzel leaned back as their coffee arrived. 'It's enough to drive a man up a tree; why in hell don't they print the man's address instead of all that silly hocus-pocus with the symbols and the numbers?'

Alvarado slowly put all the other small pictures back into his envelope as he replied. 'If they made it simple, they'd have to fire five thousand clerks, and you know they couldn't possibly do that.'

Deputy Wetzel was already beyond the matter of the symbols and numbers. As he sweetened the coffee he put a question to Alvarado. 'Is that guy I put the finger on, your fire ant-killer?'

Alvarado countered with a question of his own. 'After we met yesterday, and after you got back to Lompoc, who did you tell you'd met an L.A. detective?'

'My sergeant,' stated the deputy. 'That's all. Why?'

'Because something happened last night that made it seem as though the fire ant knew I was on his tail.'

Deputy Wetzel had his cup poised in mid-air as he listened to this. His expression became entirely innocent. 'If you mean you think that maybe someone up around my territory, me or the sergeant, fouled you up, there wouldn't be any way. Don't either of us know more than a handful of people in L.A., and those are cops, like you.'

Alvarado accepted this. 'Coincidence, then,' he told the deputy sheriff, and glanced up as a lean, boyish man approached the table dangling a pair of earphones and a chopper-pilot's small microphone in his fist.

Alvarado introduced himself, shook the pilot's hand, and would have ordered coffee for him, but the pilot did not sit down. He looked at Wetzel. 'You said it wasn't going to take more'n about a half hour.'

Wetzel responded shortly. 'It didn't. I'm finished. You in that big a hurry?'

The pilot nodded, still not smiling. Alvarado arose, and when Deputy Wetzel gulped the last of his coffee, the three of them went back out to the area with the red and white pylons. The pilot relented a little as Wetzel ducked into the plexiglas bubble. He turned towards Alvarado and said, 'You know how it is, Inspector. Rush, rush, rush. Especially this time of year.'

Alvarado nodded, stepped past to thank Deputy Wetzel for coming down, then he stepped back as the pilot climbed in and began cranking his rotors.

The only real breath of moving air which had touched George Alvarado since he'd left his office, came when the helicopter revved up. It came so strongly, in fact, that Alvarado had to retreat from it.

He lingered until the helicopter was making a clumsy, tilted, come-around before heading north up the coast, then returned to his car and drove back towards his precinct building.

The day was getting along but regardless of the distant position of the sun, that muggy, irritating smoggy-heat did not abate. Even when Alvarado was back over in his own area, which was a considerable distance from the smoke-stack pollutants, the mugginess was still noticeable. The air did not taste nor smell as badly, but the un-nerving humid heat was still there.

He went upstairs to his office, hung his jacket on the back of the door, pulled loose his tie, and for a while, just stood near the closed window allowing the coolness to soak in.

The telephone rang. It was Captain Murphy wanting to know if Alvarado was back yet, but, more to the point, he wanted to know if the helicopter had started on its return trip, which it obviously had, if Alvarado was back again in his office.

'You'd think Traffic suspected me of trying to steal their gawddamned helicopter,' said Murphy. 'They've called twice, now. Okay; that's all I wanted. I'll get back to them and tell the dispatcher we're obliged for Traffic's co-operation — and where he can shove those rotors . . . By the way — do any good?'

'Yes, I got an identification, but I just got back and haven't had t . . . '

'Do it, George, get right on it.'

'Well now what the hell did you think I was going to do, Captain; sit around here contemplating my navel?'

Murphy paused, then spoke again, softer this time. 'I forgot. You're touchy. George, you sure are touchy.'

Alvarado put down the telephone, looked exasperatedly at it, then bleakly smiled as he fished out his handkerchief to mop his neck.

He pulled out the DMV envelope, sifted through for the photograph of Donald Philip Robinson, shoved the envelope-full of other little photographs

175

into a desk drawer, and sifted through the scattered papers atop the desk until he found the rap-sheet on Donald Philip Robinson, previously furnished by Records and Files.

Robinson's most recent difficulty had arisen over an accident he had had near National City, in San Diego County, which was the last stop in the U.S. before the U.S.-Mexican border was reached. Robinson's insurance company had taken care of everything. There was a cryptic notation in someone's longhand to the effect that Donald P. Robinson had taken his eyes off the road for a moment, and had rear-ended some holidayers, very hard. That same unknown long-hander had written: 'stupid' after his last period.

Otherwise, Donald P. Robinson had a rather impressive record as a violater. He had only two convictions, two sentencings, and two records of incarceration. One of those was terminated a year short of the three year term for exemplary behaviour. Both those charges had been for smuggling. But when Alvarado leaned back to read on, expecting to read that

Robinson had been trying to smuggle narcotics through from Mexico, which was North America's major source of supply, he discovered that Robinson had been trying to smuggle in jewellers tools and supplies, for which there was a very high import duty.

The balance of the report showed that Donald Philip Robinson was a violater of almost admirable diversity. He had been arrested for suspected burglary, for receiving stolen goods, for dealing in counterfeit bank notes, and once for abduction, but that charge had been quashed at the instigation of the City Attorney's office, on the grounds that there was insufficient evidence.

Alvarado scratched his head. He picked up the little photograph and studied it for a long moment, before going back to his perusal of the rap-sheet. Robinson did not look like the kind of a man who would be so varied in his illegality, so talented in so many different felonious undertakings.

But the last run-in Robinson had had with the police had been up in San

Francisco where he had bought a car with a cheque that bounced. He subsequently made the cheque good, in cash, to the last red cent, so, although he was hauled in, again, no charges were pressed.

There was no record of any kind for the past eighteen months. Alvarado scooped up the telephone to ask if Records and Files had anything down there which had not been posted yet. The retort he got from a gravelly-voiced woman made him wince.

'We post everything the same day it comes in, and if you people up in Homicide were just *half* as efficient, people wouldn't be afraid to walk the streets at night!'

Alvarado replaced the telephone. He had not gotten a direct answer to his question, but he had most certainly got *an* answer.

He went back to reading the Robinson record. He even re-read it. Here was a busy man with a record going back more than fifteen years, without a single lapse of any length at all, until about a year and a half ago. Robinson had consistently made his living by being a criminal. And he had been a busy individual.

If it were considered that Robinson had not always been caught breaking laws, then he had been a very busy individual.

Then came the period of eighteen months when he had not even been stopped for a traffic citation.

Alvarado tossed down the file. Whatever Robinson had been involved in over the past year and a half, had to be a very smooth undertaking. It also had to be very worthwhile; Robinson had assault charges in his record, but there had been no record of any murder charge ever being filed against the man, which probably meant that Donald P. Robinson was not a killer; was at least not a man who killed out of hand.

And yet he had killed four men.

Alvarado arose, shoved everything from the top of his desk into the top drawer of the desk, locked up and took down his jacket as he headed for the door. He and Captain Murphy had predicted an identification of the fire ant by tonight. Well; there it was, in Alvarado's top desk drawer — with one glaring discrepancy; the fire ant *was* a killer, Donald Philip Robinson had never *been* a killer.

Alvarado, coat slung over one shoulder, walked down the stairs, across the foyer and out into the late-day stifling humidity. Robinson was the fire ant, he was unwilling to believe otherwise — this afternoon, anyway — and the fire ant had killed four men. The difficulty arose when Alvarado thought ahead, after the arrest of Donald Philip Robinson, to the case he had to work up for the prosecuting attorney. There had been no fingerprints, there had been no murder-weapon recovered. There was not even a motive, for Robinson to have killed those four men.

But he'd done it. Alvarado was sure of that. Robinson had knifed to death Shippen, Gomez, Holquin and Mendez, and there was not one piece of worthwhile evidence to take to the prosecuting attorney's office — which of course meant that the prosecuting attorney would flatly refuse to bring the man to trial, even for a preliminary hearing to determine possible implication.

Alvarado drove home, showered, got his glass of beer and padded barefoot out into the sitting room, but tonight he neglected to switch on the television set.

He knew exactly what was needed. He did not seriously doubt his ability to get it. What held his interest right up until he retired was the identity of this factor called motivation. Without it as the basis for the commission of a crime, there just was no way to bring a criminal to trial, and secure a conviction against him.

15

A Particular Lab Report

Alvarado saw Donald P. Robinson the afternoon following his conviction that Robinson was the fire-ant killer. It happened during the course of Alvarado's somewhat casual stake-out of the man's Westwood Village flat.

Robinson came downstairs, walked round back, got into a shiny, practically new Cadillac, and drove off in the direction of the city.

For Alvarado recognition had been easy. He could have closed his eyes and seen the man's face at any time. But he hadn't driven to Robinson's neighbourhood to make a confirmation through visual contact; he hadn't even expected to see the man, for that matter.

After Robinson's departure, Alvarado got out of his car and strolled the neighbourhood. Later, he went up to the manager's ground-floor apartment of the building where Robinson resided, and enquired about a possible vacancy. The manager, a genial, heavy-set man, said he hadn't had a vacancy in almost two years and did not anticipate one. His most recent tenant, Donald Robinson, had moved in about a year and a half ago, and otherwise, his tenants had been with him for as long as five years. Being helpful, the heavyset man then walked out a short way with Alvarado and pointed down the street where several buildings had vacancy-signs posted.

'Try down there,' he said. 'Of course those buildings are on the west side of the street, which means you'll get the sunlight first thing in the morning, unless you're lucky and talk someone out of a back apartment,' he nudged Alvarado and winked. 'Those vacancies they want to fill will be in the front of the building, I'll bet you anything.'

Alvarado smiled back. 'Glad you warned me. Nobody needs the morning sun in their eyes, especially this time of year, when it pops up about four o'clock in the morning . . . A little while ago I saw a guy drive out of here in a Cadillac. You must have some pretty solid tenants.'

The heavy-set man's reply barely avoided sounding boastful. 'Well, in this business you want to screen 'em as best you can, you see. Not because they might skip and leave you unpaid for a couple of months. That's not much of a problem when you live in your own building. But because if you get people who aren't well-established in their work, you get a lot of turnover, and that's what you particularly don't want, you see. Try and get tenants who've been on the same job four or five years, at least. If they're married, that's even better; you avoid the wild parties and stuff like that.'

Alvarado nodded. 'The guy with the Cadillac looked like a substantial tenant.'

'Well; he's not married, but he's a man who stays pretty much to himself. Travels a little, now and then. He's in lumber sales. Not a retailer, you see, a dealer; he buys carload lots from the mills up north, and sells 'em locally to the retail outlets. Must do pretty darned well at it, to drive that big black Cadillac.' The heavy-set man winked. 'Maybe that's his compensation. Everybody's got one, you see. Don Robinson — that's the guy's name, or did I say that? — he's not married, and he seems to work pretty hard, so that expensive car is his compensation. Did you ever read any of those books about psychology that're on the stands now?'

Alvarado hadn't. 'I was never smart enough to understand that stuff,' he said. 'But it sounds reasonable, this guy compensating for some of the things he's missing by owning that big car. But he must have friends, some other outlet for his needs, besides the car.'

The heavyset man shook his head. 'Of course I don't keep watch on the tenants, but I can't recall Mr. Robinson ever having more than one or two callers in all the time he's lived here. Like I said, he stays pretty much to himself.' The heavyset man turned. 'Well; I got to get back inside, the all-stars baseball game'll be coming on the television in a little while.'

Alvarado smiled. 'It's been nice talking

to you,' he said. 'Thanks for the tip about flats on the east side of the buildings.'

On his way to the parked car, Alvarado went over what he'd just been told. Some of it was interesting, even a little enlightening, but none of it provided any clues about Donald P. Robinson.

However, as much of the day as he'd used up doing a little preliminary leg-work on Robinson, certainly hadn't been wasted. On the drive back to the office he considered a stake-out. He also considered surveillance. The reason he abandoned the idea of having Robinson watched was because, up until now, he did not have anything he could use as solid evidence to warrant an arrest, and without something like that, if Robinson became suspicious and fled, there would be no valid way to stop him.

The best course of action, then, for the time being, was to keep an eye on the man's goings and comings, and otherwise not to do anything which might make him wary. Alvarado believed that Robinson would be an alert, careful, suspicious, individual.

When he got back to the office Captain Murphy arrived, bearing a laboratory report. He listened to what Alvarado had to say about Robinson, then wordlessly dropped the lab report atop the desk, and pointed at it with a rigid finger.

'You want to know who killed Mendez, Holquin and Gomez? Read that!'

There were three pages, stapled together. The first page was a very thorough report on Leslie Shippen's pearl-handled automatic pistol. But it was not a very long report for a simple reason; Shippen had bought the gun new from an arms dealer in the city whose reputation was excellent. Essentially, the report covered the time when the weapon had been serial-numbered at the factory, on through the various wholesalers and retailers who had owned it, and had passed it on until it ended up in the showcase of the dealer who had sold the gun to Shippen. After that, there was nothing, so Alvarado tossed the report aside. He was not the least bit interested in the gun *prior* to Shippen's ownership, and with nothing in the report subsequent to Shippen's acquisition of the weapon, the report was useless.

Captain Murphy strolled to the window and stood gazing out as Alvarado read the second report, which covered that rather functional, bone-handled dagger, which Alvarado had assumed Shippen perhaps used as a prop in his work.

This weapon had been handmade, from an old horseshoe rasp. The steel was better than the steel currently used in knives. Whoever had made the dagger had neglected to put any personal marking on it, which was customary. He had done an excellent job of fitting the bone handle to the steel tang of the weapon. He had also fitted the brass hilt with precise care. The weapon, according to the lab technician who had worked up the report on it, was probably fifty to sixty years old, had been made by someone who was more nearly a blacksmith than a machinist, and over the years probably a series of owners had used the blade for everything from removing old paint to hacking pieces of kindling wood for fireplaces. Further historical data, the report said, would just about have to be derived from the most recent owner of the knife, and from him on back as far as there were people living who would remember the weapon.

Alvarado looked around at Captain Murphy, whose back was to him, then tossed that report after the other one.

The final report, obviously, was what had brought Captain Murphy to Alvarado's office.

That ornate old dagger, according to the report, had been identified by the assistant curator at the Los Angeles County Museum as being originally Italian, with several subsequent alterations, one unquestionably French, the most recent one English. He placed the date of manufacture somewhere in the sixteenth century. He also dated the blade as perhaps a hundred years earlier than the handle. As for the curlicue-symbols just below the guard, he interpreted those to mean that someone named Pinocchini had created the blade in the city of Venice.

There was another long paragraph on

the history of the dagger which would no doubt have thrilled a collector of antique weapons, which Alvarado was not, so he skipped all that and resumed reading where the quotation marks stopped. Down there, near the bottom of the page, the lab technician's terse statements and short sentences stopped Alvarado in his tracks.

'There are two nicks in the blade which are scarcely noticeable to the naked eye, but they can be located by running the finger along the cutting edge. These nicks correspond exactly with imprints of knife-blade-nicks shown in frozen sections of four murder victims, supplied to this laboratory by the coroner's office . . . '

There was a little more, but Alvarado turned back to re-read this one damning paragraph. Behind him, Captain Murphy said, 'I happened to be downstairs and stopped in at the lab. They had those reports worked up at your request, so I brought them up. But you weren't in, so I took them on up to my office and read them.'

Alvarado arose from the desk, paced almost to the door, paced back, then picked up the telephone to call Fisk at the coroner's office. When Fisk was on the line Alvarado said, 'I'm going to send an old dagger down to you. We believe it's the weapon used to kill Shippen, Holquin, Gomez and Mendez. Our lab's run tests and has come up with this idea. I'd like to have you do the same, really to authenticate that this is the murder weapon. All right?'

Fisk agreed. 'Yes, of course. And you can rely absolutely on our report.'

Alvarado, always annoyed by assumptions of superiority, said, 'Yeah,' and put down the telephone as he raised his eyes to Gerald Murphy.

The captain returned Alvarado's stare as he said, 'If Robinson killed Shippen, then he wiped off the damned dagger and put it in the desk drawer, before departing.'

'What do you mean, *if*,' demanded Alvarado. 'That's the only way he could have done it.'

Captain Murphy inclined his head.

'Okay; but now you've got something else — did Robinson bring the dagger with him, or was it already in Shippen's apartment — and if it was already there, George, then there's one hell of a big possibility that Robinson didn't kill Holquin, Mendez and Gomez — Shippen killed them.'

The telephone rang. It was Elisabeth Fraser, who asked in a very pleasant, calm tone of voice if Inspector Alvarado had made any progress in his investigation of her stolen nude. Before Alvarado answered, he stood a moment narrowly studying Captain Murphy, then, with his gaze clearing, turning cold and speculative, he said, 'I'll drive out this afternoon and personally report. All right?'

She laughed. 'All right. I'll welcome the company. I've made a discovery about myself; I'd make a terrible hermit . . . hermitess?'

Alvarado leaned down to replace the phone, telling Captain Murphy who his caller had been. Then he glanced up. 'Jerry, when I got into Shippen's studio, there was nothing atop his desk but an address book, some artist's catalogues, and the telephone.'

'What of it?'

'Suppose that old dagger was on the desk, Jerry. Suppose it was there, and Robinson saw it, picked it up and killed Shippen with it.'

'Well . . . ' said Murphy, looking puzzled.

'Jerry, if the knife was on the desk *before Shippen was killed by it*, only two living people would know that — the killer and Elisabeth Fraser, who was in the studio before, *and after* the murder. If Robinson cleaned the knife and shoved it into a desk-drawer after he killed Shippen, she should possibly remember that the knife was no longer on the desk when she came out of the bedroom.'

Captain Murphy pondered this for a moment before saying, 'Okay; go out and see what she remembers. Just tell me one thing: If the damned dagger was on the desk before Robinson arrived . . . ?'

Alvarado straightened up as he answered. 'Then my guess is that *Shippen* was the fire ant, the guy who killed

Holquin, Mendez and Gomez, not Robinson. If not, then tell me what the hell he was doing with that murder-knife in his possession . . . Jerry; send someone down to the coroner's office with the dagger will you?'

Alvarado did not wait for the answer from Captain Murphy as he went out the door heading for the stairs.

The day was well along towards being spent, but this time of year daylight would linger long after the sun departed. In fact, this time of year, the coolest, most pleasant time of day, excluding dawn, was the lingering, long periods of pleasant dusk. Alvarado drove to Sorrel Lane well ahead of the dusk, but he would not leave Sorrel Lane until long after dusk had arrived.

16

Alvarado's Anxieties

Alvarado was climbing out of the car when he remembered something, and settled back in again, reaching for the dashboard transceiver. He put in a call to Captain Murphy, got his secretary instead, and asked that a very discreet stake-out be put upon the residence of Donald P. Robinson. He gave the address, waited until this had been confirmed, then finally left the car, angling across the expanse of neatly clipped grass towards the Spanish-style patio.

He expected to be intercepted, and he was. This time by a pug-nosed, red-headed detective who seemed to know Alvarado by sight, because he held out a hand while saying, 'Your ID please, Inspector.'

Alvarado was silent. This time, he was not in a frame of mind for banter. When the folder was handed back, he nodded and paced on up to the patio, and to the door on the far side of it.

Elisabeth Fraser admitted him, wearing a jacket and slacks which matched, grey, with a thin white stripe. She looked immaculate, as usual, and she smiled as though their last meeting had not come close to ending with sparks.

She studied him a moment, while closing the door, then said, 'You look tired, Inspector.'

He could have answered that, but instead he got to the reason for his visit. 'Mrs. Fraser, how long did you sit for Shippen the morning he was killed?'

She moved towards the sofa as she replied. 'How long? I would guess perhaps an hour, possibly a little longer.' She sat down, leaned with both arms on her knees, hands clasped, gazing up at him. 'We usually took breaks; sometimes we'd have a cup of coffee, sometimes he would go on working, and I'd glance through a magazine until he was ready to go again.'

'That particular morning, Mrs. Fraser,

you didn't leave the studio, during your breaks?'

'No.'

'Well then,' said Alvarado, having led up to his point. 'For an hour or more you were in the studio. While you were posing, facing the north wall of the room, could you see the desk?'

She got a slight, straight line across her forehead as she answered. 'Of course; it was slightly to my left, but in front of me.'

'Can you recall what was on the desk, Mrs. Fraser?'

She frowned a little more, and glanced at her clasped hands before speaking. 'Yes, I think so. There were some booklets, one or two typed pages, of course, and an old dagger, which I assumed Leslie used as a letter-opener.'

Alvarado kept anything from showing on his face. 'And afterwards, Mrs. Fraser, when you came out fully clothed and found Mr. Shippen dead on the floor, by any chance did you look at the things on the desk again?'

She suddenly shot him a wide-eyed look. 'The dagger,' she murmured.

'You're talking about the dagger, aren't you?'

'Yes. Was it there, afterwards?'

Her answer nearly cancelled-out his earlier feeling of exultation. 'I don't remember whether it was or not. I didn't go over to the desk, Inspector. I — was too shaken up. It was there during the posing, I know that for a fact, but afterwards . . . Well, I ran out of the apartment, as I told you.' She stared at him. 'I'm sorry.'

He was also sorry. That had been his second most crucial question. She had answered the first one perfectly, but not the second one. He went to a chair, sat down and stared at the portrait of her on the front wall, without really seeing it. If there had been fingerprints on the old dagger. But there hadn't been, according to the lab report. If there had been verification that the knife had been moved by the only other person known to have been there, immediately *after* the slaying . . . But that wasn't verifiable now, either.

She said, 'Inspector, do you know who stole my portrait from the studio?'

He nodded a little indifferently. 'I think so, yes.'

'Then you know who killed Leslie.'

He looked over at her. 'I *suspect* who killed him, but that's not the same as *knowing*. You can't put a man on trial for what you *suspect*.'

She continued to sit with her knees together, her arms resting upon them, hands clasped in front of her. 'Was he killed with that old dagger?'

Alvarado did not decline to answer her question out of professionalism, which would have been correct for him. He simply did not answer it because he had another question for her.

'Had you ever seen that knife in the studio before, Mrs. Fraser?'

'No. Not that I recall. From time to time Leslie used props, perhaps a bowl of fruit, an arrangement of flowers, but I don't remember him ever using the knife at all.' She raised her eyes. 'In fact, while he never showed me *all* his oils, the ones that I have seen did not have any weapons in them. Certainly not that dagger, or I'd have remembered seeing it before. Inspector, his specialisation was people, not things, not objects like other artists paint. He was matchless as a portrayer of people. Look at that half-profile he did of me; I don't know how he ever managed to capture that exact expression. I'm not an introspective person, I'm almost never sad nor poignant. But that's what he saw, and he brought it out beautifully, don't you think?'

Alvarado nodded without looking at the portrait. He was not interested in Leslie Shippen's genius, he was interested in his murder.

What he had hoped to do, and what he had failed at, was to link Robinson with Shippen by the knife. All he had succeeded in doing was link *Shippen* to the knife. The damned thing *had* been atop his desk prior to the slaying; it was the same knife used to kill Holquin, Mendez and Gomez, and that linked Shippen, who was dead, to those other three dead men.

If the knife had *not* been on the desk *after* the murder, then either Elisabeth

Fraser, who was not even a suspect, or Donald Robinson who *was* a suspect, had wiped the thing off and put in into the desk drawer.

The fact that it had been in the drawer when Alvarado first found it, proved that someone had put it there, probably Robinson, but that was not good enough to support a direct allegation against Robinson. If Elisabeth had seen the damned thing before, and had *not* seen it afterwards . . . but that hope had just gone out the window.

Alvarado arose, looking slightly morose. The beautiful woman arose, too. In a tone full of sincerity, she said, 'I'd give anything to be able to help you, Inspector.'

He smiled at her. 'Thanks. You've helped. At least the knife was there before the murder. That's worth something.' He continued to gaze down into her lifted face. 'I'm not quite sure what it's worth, but it's got to be worth something.'

She grinned at his rueful humour and accompanied him across to the vicinity of the door. 'I'm a disappointment to you, aren't I?'

He reached for the knob while looking at her. What she had just said, gave him a perfect opportunity to be gallant, and he wanted to be, but Captain Murphy's remonstrance popped into the forefront of his mind, so all he said was something neutral, and got out of there.

He wasn't halted on his way to the parked car, and it didn't occur to him that this had not happened until he was leaning to punch the starter. He remained leaning forward a moment, peering back across the dusky garden until he saw the thick, vague shape fade out along the north corner of the house, then he gunned the car to life, made an illegal U-turn in the centre of the square, and drove off in the direction of his apartment building.

This was another of those nights when he went through his habitual routine, right up to the point of where he usually switched on the television set. Tonight, as he had done the previous night, he simply sat there, beer glass in hand, staring at the big blank eye and did not turn the set on.

The following morning he did not awaken with any brilliant ideas. In fact, by the time he was ready to leave the flat for his car, he did not feel much different, good night's rest notwithstanding, than he had felt when he had departed from the house on Sorrel Lane the evening before.

When he reached the office he still did not feel very encouraged. There were several reports on the desktop from the surveillance teams. There was also a note from the stake-out personnel on Robinson's building. The men on Robinson noted cryptically that their principal had arrived home at eight o'clock in the evening, had gone into his apartment, and had not re-emerged throughout the entire night. The report on the Sorrel Lane residence was the same, except for one notation; shortly after the night-shift had taken over from the day-shift, it had been noted that a dark Cadillac had cruised past the Sorrel Lane house twice, once travelling northward, and again, about a half hour later travelling southward.

Alvarado re-read that, then picked up the other report, the one saying that Robinson had not left his apartment all night. Either Robinson *had* left, or it was another damned coincidence. He was inclined to believe that's what it was, too. Cadillacs were in fact fairly common in the residential areas of Beverly Hills, which was an affluent community. He made a notation to have the car stopped if it cruised past again, then he acted on a hunch, he called downstairs to speak to the man who had typed up the Sorrel Lane report. When he had that detective on the line he asked about a licence number. The answer confirmed the value of hunches.

'I couldn't really see it, Inspector, which is why I didn't put it in the report. Those damned yellow numbers against a dark blue background may be aesthetic as all hell, but they're just about impossible to read from any distance at night. They ought to reverse it, have the background yellow and the numbers blue. I think there were some letters as a prefix, maybe like DEC, something like that, but . . . '

'Maybe DEF?' asked Alvarado.

'Yeah, it could have been DEF. But like I said . . . '

Alvarado interrupted to say, 'Thanks,' and rang off. He carefully pencilled in the DEF prefix on the detective's report, then tossed down the pen and leaned far back in his chair.

If that *had* been a DEF prefix, then either those men on the Robinson stake-out had gone to sleep on the job, or the DEF Cadillac on Sorrel Lane hadn't been Robinson.

There was a way to double-check. He arose and left the office outward bound. It was still morning when he drove away, in the direction of the Robinson residence, and therefore it was still cool. But the traffic was deadly. He used up almost a full hour going about seven miles.

This time, he approached the building without a ruse, went around back to the garages, located the one with the name D. P. Robinson under the overhead light outside, and was rewarded, first, by finding the garage was empty, and, secondly, by being approached from the adjoining yard by a compact man who walked like a cat. He eyed the man, did not recognise him, and pulled out his ID folder as he said, 'How long ago did the car from this stall pull out?'

The compact man responded with an immediate answer. 'Half hour ago. I was just writing it up in my notebook for the daily report. I'm Hallam from the downstairs pool, Inspector.' Hallam smiled. He seemed to be a pleasant, disarming man. 'The guy came out with an attaché case and drove off, just like he did yesterday morning, regular as clockwork.'

'The report for last night says he didn't leave after coming home,' stated Alvarado.

Hallam nodded. 'Yeah, I know. The night-man was writing it up when I came on duty at five this morning.'

'There's reason to believe he *did* leave, Hallam.'

The detective's gaze at Alvarado did not waver. 'No way, Inspector. The guy who was on him last night doesn't make mistakes like that. I know; I've worked with him for two years. If he said the principal didn't leave, you can damned well believe it.'

'Maybe it was just his car, then.'

'I doubt that, too, Inspector. When I came on duty this morning, I went in and looked at it. The bonnet was cold, the car hadn't been driven since the day before . . . Inspector, I think someone gave you a bum steer.'

Alvarado toyed with the idea of talking to the heavyset man who ran the apartment building, but gave it up. Detective Hallam had been adequately convincing. His original purpose, though, had been to talk to the heavyset man.

It *had* been a coincidence, then. He could have returned to his office to see whether any of the other owners of dark Cadillacs on the DEF list lived anywhere near Sorrel Lane, but he didn't; he was satisfied it hadn't been Robinson, and that was all that really mattered.

As he climbed back into the car, a little disgusted, he told himself that it was precisely this kind of a damned situation that made police work most exasperating. Then he decided to visit the house on Sorrel Lane again, just to make certain everything was all right.

17

Exposé

He encountered the big, solid detective again, after leaving his car, bound for the patio of the house on Sorrel Lane, but this time the encounter was brief. The detective passed Alvarado along with only a glance at his ID.

But Alvarado had a question. 'By any chance, since you've been on duty, has a dark Cadillac cruised past?'

The big man shook his head. 'No. Not that I saw, Inspector, and I've been watching what little traffic uses this street.'

Alvarado said, 'Thanks,' and went on up to the house.

Elisabeth Fraser admitted him with a smile. 'You're just in time, Inspector. I was having coffee and I don't like sitting there alone.' She took him to a small alcove off the kitchen, which was a sunshiny little breakfast nook, sat him down at the table, and went into the kitchen to get his coffee. Through the connecting, doorless archway she was in his view all the time she worked. This morning she was wearing a pale cotton dress that couldn't have been tailored for her, but certainly looked as though it had. When she turned and caught him looking at her, she smiled.

'You're in a slightly better mood this morning, Inspector, but not altogether,' she said, and came forth with his cup and saucer. 'I think you need a vacation.'

He blinked, but did not mention that he was due to begin his annual holiday the following week.

The coffee was excellent, which he told her, adding that he'd never been able to make a good cup of coffee in his life.

'You're not supposed to be able to,' was her retort. 'That requires a woman's touch.'

He considered that a moment before speaking. 'You're not a liberated woman, then? I mean, you like doing domestic things?'

She laughed. 'I'm liberated. I'm self-employed, keep my own flat, my own car, spend my own money.' Her grey-green gaze considered him with amusement. 'But liberation means doing things you want to do, doesn't it? I happen to enjoy domestic things.'

He decided to change the subject; for some reason, every time he visited the house on Sorrel Lane, something like this cropped up, something that offered him all sorts of opportunities to put their acquaintanceship on a basis which was not professional. Not that he really objected, but it made him slightly uneasy.

'Anything interesting happen round here last night?' he asked, and she continued to gaze at him, but with the warmth dwindling.

'Nothing. How could it, with a phalanx of Philistines tramping through the flowerbeds?'

He grinned, and drained the coffee cup. She offered him a re-fill, which he declined. Then she said, 'I've been thinking,' and because he'd heard this from amateurs at least once a month ever since he'd been in Homicide, he sighed.

'I've been thinking, Inspector Alvarado, that Leslie must have put that dagger atop the desk for some particular purpose, either the night before he was murdered, or the same morning. I've been sitting for him for over a year, and I'd never seen it there before, have never seen any kind of weapon on the desk or in the studio, before. Do you suppose he knew that man was coming to see him, and expected trouble?'

Alvarado's answer was terse. 'Mrs. Fraser, there was a new, fully loaded, automatic pistol in a desk drawer. If you anticipated trouble, which would you put out to use, a very efficient automatic, or an antique dagger?'

She lowered her eyes to the cup in front of her. 'You're right, of course.' The greeny eyes swept up again. 'Then why *did* he put it there?'

Alvarado answered this question in the same dry tone. 'That's indeed something to think about — but the point is, how do I identify the man who killed Shippen with it?'

She sat thoughtfully regarding him, then she said, 'You told me you knew who killed him.'

'I said I *suspected* who killed him, Mrs. Fraser, and that's all it can be, until I have some kind of proof.'

'That's a technicality, Inspector.'

'Yeah, it sure is, and that's how courts of law function, on technicalities. I once saw something to that effect engraved on a plaque.'

She arose to get herself another cup of coffee. As she passed through into the kitchen she asked if he wouldn't change his mind and join her in another cup, and he relented. She returned for his cup, smiled and said, 'I don't envy you your job. Don't they have something engraved outside your building about the frustrations of police work?'

He smiled up at her, started to answer, then sat stone still. She saw the astonishment cross his face, saw his eyes drift away from her, and although she hesitated, watching, finally, she turned and went back to get them both a second cup of coffee, leaving him alone until she returned, then, as she sat down, she said, 'Well . . . ?'

His response was not very enlightening — at first. 'Do you remember something you said to me on my first visit out here, when you were showing me that portrait Shippen did of you, that's hanging in the sitting room?'

She looked blankly across the table. 'No.'

'You said, 'it's like an engraving, isn't it?''

'I did?'

Alvarado pushed the cup aside and leaned on the table. 'Shippen was arrested once for being implicated in the forgery of race-track tickets. Robinson was arrested once for being involved in counterfeiting. Do you see the connection?'

She answered candidly. 'No.'

He arose, went to the telephone, called Captain Murphy and asked that someone be sent out to Robinson's address to meet him. Murphy's answer to that was brusque. '*I'll* meet you. What's up?'

'I've still got that John Doe arrest

warrant. What I really need is a search warrant, but maybe the John Doe warrant will work. I want a look inside Robinson's flat.'

'Why?' demanded Murphy.

'Because I think I've got the connection between Shippen and Robinson — either forgery or counterfeiting. I've been all over Shippen's place, so if there's equipment, it's got to be at the Robinson place.'

'Yeah,' said Murphy, 'unless they've got it cached somewhere else. All right; I'll meet you at the Robinson apartment in an hour — *with* a search warrant. Damned if I'm going to stick *my* neck out!'

As Alvarado replaced the telephone, Elisabeth Fraser arose from the table to stare at him. 'Leslie was a forger, Inspector, a counterfeiter?'

'*Someone* was, Mrs. Fraser. I'm betting on it.'

'It's hard to believe,' she murmured, 'but I know one thing — he did do an occasional engraving.'

Alvarado turned. 'You didn't mention that before.'

'Why should I? I had no idea it meant anything. He had three or four very good engravings. He showed them to me last year, but I haven't seen them around the studio since, so I suppose he sold them.'

Alvarado said, 'Thanks for the coffee,' and started for the front door. She went with him, let him out, and he hardly more than nodded as he struck out for his parked car.

There was something else he now recalled, which hadn't seemed very important when he'd read of it on Robinson's rap-sheet: That time Robinson was apprehended smuggling jeweller's supplies and tools into the country from Mexico.

On the drive to Robinson's apartment he put it all together, and it came out exactly as he had first guessed; either as forgery or as counterfeiting. He was ready to swear at himself, too, for not having surmised that someone with Shippen's artistic ability, and Shippen's dishonest background, wouldn't be involved in something which he could do so well. The best engravers were artists; the best

216

counterfeiting plates were made by professional engravers!

He reached the Robinson apartment building in time to see Captain Murphy out front in conversation with Hallam, the detective on stake-out with whom Alvarado had discussed the possibility of Robinson leaving his flat the previous evening. As Alvarado left his car and started forward, the heavyset manager of the building came to his front door, gazing with obvious curiosity out where two men were conferring, and a third man was hastening forward to join them.

Captain Murphy turned towards Alvarado. 'Robinson's not home.' Murphy fished inside his jacket and flourished a crisp, folded paper. 'Here's your search warrant. You ready?'

Alvarado nodded, took the warrant, and started up where the heavyset man was standing, scowling. The scowl did not lift when Alvarado held out his ID folder, then showed the search warrant. It did not lift even when the heavyset man looked accusingly at Alvarado, and said, 'So you were a cop all the time.'

Alvarado ignored that. 'Do you have a pass-key to the Robinson apartment?'

'Yes. Right here in my pocket.'

'Then let's go,' stated Alvarado, and moved aside for the heavyset man to lead the way. But first the heavyset man had to glower at Captain Murphy, asking who *he* was. Murphy showed his folder, and finally, with a grunt, the heavyset man led the way. As he tromped up the stairs, holding to a railing, he grunted again, not, Alvarado assumed, from the climb, but because he was still surprised, and irritated.

The door to Robinson's flat yielded easily to the pass-key. The heavyset man stepped aside for the detectives to move inside first, then he padded after them.

The sitting room was drab. The entire apartment smelled stale, there was not a window open anywhere. There was a cubby-hole kitchen and dinette, neither of which were very clean, and there was a master bedroom, with an un-made bed in it, and a man's clothing draped from two chairs. The second bedroom door only yielded when the pass-key was used again.

Alvarado and Murphy stopped just inside, leaving the heavyset man to crane past them at the small, electric printing press, the steel work-bench with implements scattered over it, the lay-out of engraving plates, and the stack of neatly trimmed papers beside a paper-knife upon a smaller table.

Alvarado walked over, picked up one of the plates, examined it without speaking, and handed it to Captain Murphy, who said, 'Twenty dollar notes. What's that other plate for?'

'Tens,' said Alvarado, and, remembering something from the stake-out report about Robinson departing this morning with an attaché case, sifted through three drawers under the metal work-bench until he found them — stacks of newly-printed, seemingly flawless, green bank notes in the denominations engraved upon the plates.

Captain Murphy came over, looked, and straightened back. 'Well; we've got something for the Treasury Department,' he said. 'But that's not going to do us much good, is it?'

Alvarado didn't answer. He studied the printing press, the engraved plates, the lay-out of tools, and finally he turned towards the heavyset man. 'Lumber dealer?' he said, quietly.

The heavyset man recoiled. 'My gawd — that's what he told me. I had no idea . . . Listen, if I'd had any idea at all he was doing something like this . . . ' The heavyset man backed clear as Alvarado walked out of the room. 'I'll arrange to have a detective stay in your apartment with you,' Alvarado said. 'Just to keep you honest.'

'I wouldn't tell him you've been in here,' the big man said in protest. 'I believe in law and order.'

Alvarado motioned. 'Let's go back downstairs.'

Captain Murphy was the last man out. He locked the door after them, and followed Alvarado to the ground-floor, where he went out front and called Hallam in. At the manager's door he said, 'Keep an eye on this guy. Don't let him get near a window or the door, or his telephone.'

The heavyset man was still quaking, still protesting, as Captain Murphy and George Alvarado walked back out into the sunshine.

Alvarado spoke after a long moment of thought. 'He took a load out this morning in an attaché case to distribute. If we're lucky, he dumped the counterfeit in the city and will be back this evening. I'll wait, Captain.'

Murphy was agreeable. 'I'll contact the Treasury Department.'

'Just tell them to stay away until I've contacted you that Robinson's shown up.'

Murphy nodded and briskly walked out to his car.

18

Robinson In The Net

Alvarado had never liked this particular kind of a stake out, and he did not like this one. For one thing, the apartment smelled stale, for another thing, if the detective downstairs with the heavyset man made one slight mistake, and the heavyset man was in any way sympathetic to Robinson, the counterfeiter-killer was going to escape.

Alvarado could have called in for men to stake-out the building from across the street and from around back, but that was risky. He did not want any slip-ups, so he stood by the curtained upstairs front window letting the long day wind down.

Patience was one thing a detective learned to develop, but hunger was something more basic; by early afternoon Alvarado could have eaten a raw horse. He was tempted to make a pot of coffee in Robinson's cubby-hole kitchen, and he was also tempted to open one of the cans of meat out there. Instead, he listened to his stomach grumble, eyed his watch from time to time, and waited.

He could have called in for an all-points-bulletin to be put out on the dark Cadillac, but that too, entailed risk. He preferred giving Robinson all the rope the man would need. He did not want anything to make the man suspicious, and for that he would have to pay in personal discomfort.

At two o'clock he was summoned to the telephone by a call from Captain Murphy, who had not been idle, it seemed. 'The Treasury people have been on the trail of damned near perfect tens and twenties in our area for almost two years. They were pleased as punch that we've probably busted the mystery.'

Alvarado said, 'What do you mean — *probably* busted it?'

'They won't be able to say for certain until they've compared some of those notes in the bedroom with samples they've got in their files.' Captain Murphy paused, then said, 'But hell, we've busted it all right . . . How are you doing?'

'Slowly starving to death,' responded Alvarado.

'Suppose this clown doesn't come back tonight? Maybe we'd ought to put out a bulletin on him.'

'No,' exclaimed Alvarado. 'No bulletin and no stake-out. He'll come back sooner or later. I'll wait him out.'

'Okay; incidentally, a man named Fisk called from the coroner's office; you were right, that old dagger was used in the Holquin, Gomez and Mendez homicides. They're sending it back so we can enter it as evidence.'

Alvarado heard a car turn up into the driveway out front, cut the conversation short with a curt comment about this, put down the telephone and stepped through into the master-bedroom, on the rear of the apartment, and looked out a window.

The black Cadillac was in its stall. A man carrying an attaché case was briskly walking around towards the front entrance of the building.

Alvarado's hunger vanished, and so did

his boredom as he loosened his jacket, flipped the restraining snap off his revolver, and walked quietly over to the front door, taking up a position against the wall where the door, swinging inward, would hide him.

He heard the solid footsteps leave the stairs and start along the hallway. When a key was inserted in the door-latch, he drew his revolver. The door swung inward, a man walked past, his back to Alvarado, turned to glance out the front window, then he flung the attaché case upon a sofa — and Alvarado pushed the door away. It made a slight noise and the man turned.

Alvarado knew the face and, even the somewhat thick, dumpy build. 'Don't move, Mr. Robinson. Keep your hands away from your sides.'

The astonished older man's shock held him completely motionless. Alvarado was sure his initiative had neutralised Robinson, and was taking one more forward step when Robinson suddenly hurled himself straight towards the door, which was half open. Alvarado kicked out, slammed the door with his foot, and it caught Robinson all along one side of his hurtling body. Robinson went sideways, struck a chair, and broke it as he fell with it.

Alvarado did not wait. He jumped across the room, leaned and grabbed one of Robinson's arms with his left hand, twisted the arm up between the older man's shoulderblades, and stomped, hard, on the other out-flung arm. In that awkward position, he shoved the cold gun-muzzle against Robinson's neck.

'I said — don't move!'

Robinson was gasping from pain. He made no further struggle as Alvarado yanked up the other arm and handcuffed both wrists from behind, then stepped clear, holstered his weapon, and ordered the prisoner to get to his feet. Robinson made a feeble effort but Alvarado had to help him rise. He pushed Robinson into a chair, went to the telephone and called Captain Murphy. Afterwards, he relaxed slightly, and faced his prisoner.

Robinson was still in pain. 'You broke my gawddamn ribs,' he told Alvarado. 'I can hardly breathe. That damned door hit me right in the . . . '

'You'll live,' stated the detective, studying his captive. 'You'll survive, Robinson, and that's better than can be said for the men you killed — Gomez, Holquin, Mendez and Leslie Shippen.'

Robinson's eyes widened. 'What are you talking about? I didn't kill anyone. Anyway, I got my rights.' He flicked a quick look towards the locked bedroom door. 'What right you got even being in here?'

Alvarado showed his John Doe warrant, then stuffed it back into a pocket. 'We've looked at your counter-feiting set-up. It's very good. Too bad you had to kill the goose that was laying the golden eggs. Shippen, who made your engravings.'

'I told you, damn it, I didn't kill anyone, and you can't prove I did!'

Alvarado thinly smiled. 'I can prove it. I've got the dagger used to kill them all, all four of them. I've got something else . . . what did you do with the painting of the girl who was in the apartment, that morning?'

Robinson paled a little, shot a look out the window, then sat dourly for a moment before speaking again. When he resumed, his tone had changed, had turned quieter, and sly.

'The picture's in the boot of my car. All right, I killed Shippen. But it was self-defence. But *he* killed those other guys.'

'Why would he do that?'

'Because they were distributing for us, they were passing the tens and twenties in south Los Angeles, where Shippen and I figured the Feds would think someone was making them. It was a good set-up, until Les decided, since he was furnishing the plates, he should have more of the clean money we were picking up each time one of the phoney notes was pushed. He tried to get the three beaners to go in with him against me. I was the guy who supplied them with the counterfeits, so they decided to work with me, and to help me cut Les out. He got them to go up north with him so's he could paint their picture — that was his excuse for getting them up there, away from me

— but they told me what he was trying to do, so I trailed them. We had it out, up there by Lompoc. The beaners went home. A couple of days later he struck. I didn't know anything about it until I saw the newspapers.'

'How did he contact those three in the first place?'

'Through some guy at a modelling agency,' said Robinson, and Alvarado, remembering his hunch that he should follow up something like this, winced. Robinson glanced up. 'I went to Les's studio that morning to try and get him to quit ruining our set-up. He had that damned dagger on the desk. He grabbed for it, and I grabbed him, got the dagger away from him, and when he jumped on me, I let him have it.' Robinson paused, licked his lips, then went on. 'The damned girl . . . I didn't even think to look in the other rooms. I just cleaned off the knife, shoved it in a desk drawer, and got the hell out of there. Then I remembered the painting he'd been working on. He always worked with live models. He told me that a dozen times.

That meant the girl in the picture was in the apartment.'

'So you went back, stole the painting to use in identifying the girl, and if you'd found her you'd have killed her, too.'

Robinson was uncomfortable. 'You got a cigarette?' he asked, and when Alvarado shook his head, Robinson motioned with his head. 'Reach in my pocket and light me one . . . My whole damned left side is sore.'

Alvarado lit the cigarette, plugged it between Robinson's lips, went to the telephone to call Captain Murphy, and afterwards, when his prisoner wanted a drink of water, Alvarado provided that, too. Then he sat down to wait.

Robinson was no longer agitated. He smoked, gazed at George Alvarado, and after a while he said, 'with Les Shippen it was self-defence, and you'll never make anything else out of it. So what've you got me on — a lousy charge of counterfeiting. That's five to ten years. I can live with that.' He blew smoke in Alvarado's direction. 'And I'll tell you something else; I'm going to deny everything I just told you; I'm going to say you made me talk under duress. You see, cop, I been through this before.'

Alvarado did not argue the point. All he said was, 'Yeah, I know you've been through it all before. And Robinson, that's what's going to ruin your chances for parole this time. You're going up against a Federal rap as a long-timer violater. There is one thing that might help you, though.'

'What's that?'

'The full story of Shippen killing those three *Chicanos*.'

'I'd tell that anyway,' exclaimed Robinson. 'That lousy son of a bitch — look what he did to the sweetest operation a man ever had. For almost two years we've had it all our way. And look what he did to all that!'

Alvarado heard a car stop out front and went to the window to watch Captain Murphy and two uniformed officers alight and stride briskly up the walk. He turned. 'Your escort is coming, Robinson.' He walked closer and said, 'You're a lucky man. If you'd come anywhere close to that girl, take my word for it, you'd have ended up weighted down with lead.'

Captain Murphy shoved open the door, looked at the handcuffed man in the chair, and didn't even speak to him, he simply jerked his thumb over his shoulder, and the pair of uniformed officers hoisted Robinson from the chair and took him, swearing, out of the building.

Murphy then smiled at Alvarado. 'Remember what I said: I knew you could do it within two weeks. Day after tomorrow will be Friday — the end of the second week.'

'And next Monday my holiday begins,' retorted Alvarado.

Captain Murphy did not dispute this. 'Okay, but you want to know what I think? I don't think you're going up to the high-country lakes for any fishing.'

Alvarado studied the square face and small, bright eyes of the older man in front of him. 'No? Why won't I?'

Captain Murphy did not answer. In fact, he never did answer. He jerked his head and said, 'Come along, let's go back downstairs. The Treasury agents should be showing up soon. They'll want a preliminary statement from you, as investigating officer, then they'll want you with them as a witness when they take away the junk in that locked bedroom.'

As they were returning to the lower floor, Alvarado said, 'Why won't I be going to the mountain lakes, fishing?'

Hallam, who was standing in the doorway of the heavyset man's apartment, accosted Captain Murphy with a question. 'You guys nail Robinson?'

Murphy answered. 'Yeah. He's already on his way to headquarters. What about your man?'

'Aw, he's all right; sweating like a bull in rutting season, but he's all right. The guy has already worried off ten pounds. He didn't know anything was going on.'

Murphy accepted this, and jerked his thumb over one shoulder. 'Stay with George, will you, and lend a hand when the Treasury agents get here.' As Murphy strolled on out of the building, Alvarado raised a hand, then started to call after him, but Murphy kept right on walking, and closed the street door after himself.

Hallam, looking at Alvarado, said, 'What's wrong?'

George couldn't give a very intelligent answer, so he gave none, just shrugged, and started to turn when the telephone in the heavyset man's apartment rang. Alvarado and Hallam were starting back upstairs when the heavyset man poked his head out the door and barked.

'Alvarado! You're wanted on the phone in my apartment!'

Mystified, Alvarado went back, was taken to the phone by the heavyset man, and the moment he spoke his name, Murphy's sly look made sense. Elisabeth Fraser was on the other end of the connection.

'Inspector, I tried to call you earlier, and was put through to Captain Murphy. He was wonderfully co-operative. He told me you were closing in on Leslie's killer, and that I needn't consider myself in danger any longer. Inspector . . . ?'

'Yes.'

'I was wondering — do you like homecooked meals? Captain Murphy said he knew that you did, and I'm bursting

234

with curiosity about everything that's been happening . . . Could you make it about seven this evening?'

Alvarado, under the heavyset man's suspicious stare, smiled and said 'Yes,' again, then rang off, because Hallam was motioning from the hallway; the Treasury agents had arrived.

THE END

We do hope that you have enjoyed reading this large print book.

Did you know that all of our titles are available for purchase?

We publish a wide range of high quality large print books including:
Romances, Mysteries, Classics
General Fiction
Non Fiction and Westerns

Special interest titles available in large print are:
The Little Oxford Dictionary
Music Book, Song Book
Hymn Book, Service Book

Also available from us courtesy of Oxford University Press:
Young Readers' Dictionary
(large print edition)
Young Readers' Thesaurus
(large print edition)

For further information or a free brochure, please contact us at:
Ulverscroft Large Print Books Ltd.,
The Green, Bradgate Road, Anstey,
Leicester, LE7 7FU, England.
Tel: (00 44) **0116 236 4325**
Fax: (00 44) **0116 234 0205**

DEATH CALLED AT NIGHT

R. A. Bennett

Jimmy Ellis believes his parents have died in a car crash when as a young boy he is taken to live with relatives in Australia. The years pass happily, then the nightmare comes. Terrifying images flit through his mind in the dark — all through the eyes of a child, a witness to grisly events seventeen years before. He begins to delve into the past, and soon he finds himself on the trail of a double murderer — a murderer who is prepared to kill again.

THE DEAD TALE-TELLERS

John Newton Chance

Jonathan Blake always kept appoint-
ments. He had kept many, in all sorts
of places, at all sorts of times, but
never one like that one he kept in the
house in the woods in the fading light
of an October day. It seemed a perfect,
peaceful place to visit and perhaps
take tea and muffins round the fire.
But at this appointment his footsteps
dragged, for he knew that inside the
house the men with whom he had that
date were already dead . . .

THREE DAYS TO LIVE

Robert Charles

Mike Harrigan was scar-faced, a drifter, and something of a woman-hater. With his partner Dan Barton he searched the upper reaches of the Rio Negro in the treacherous rain forests of Brazil, lured by a fortune in uncut emeralds. Behind them rode three killers who believed that they had already found the precious stones. And then fate handed Harrigan not emeralds, but the lives of women, three of them nuns, and trapped them all in a vast series of underground caverns.

THE MURDER MAKERS

John Newton Chance

Julian Hammer wrote thrillers. When people asked him how he thought of all the murders, he would reply that he did them personally first. Thus, when Jonathan Blake called on Hammer to look into the case of a missing person, it did appear that the author might have killed him. Hammer, twisting by habit, twisted the issue so well Blake began to suspect that it was Hammer who was in line to be murdered. But Hammer thought it was likely to be Blake. Both were dead right.

SEA VENGEANCE

Robert Charles

Chief Officer John Steele was disillusioned with his ship; the *Shantung* was the slowest old tramp on the China Seas, and her Captain was another fading relic. The *Shantung* sailed from Saigon, the port of war-torn Vietnam, and was promptly hijacked by the Viet Cong. John Steele, helped by the lovely but unpredictable Evelyn Ryan, gave them a much tougher fight than they had expected, but it was Captain Butcher who exacted a final, terrible vengeance.

THE CALIGARI COMPLEX

Basil Copper

Mike Faraday, the laconic L.A. private investigator, is called in when macabre happenings threaten the Martin-Hannaway Corporation. Fires, accidents and sudden death are involved; one of the partners, James Hannaway, inexplicably fell off a monster crane. Mike is soon entangled in a web of murder, treachery and deceit and through it all a sinister figure flits; something out of a nightmare. Who is hiding beneath the mask of Cesare, the somnambulist? Mike has a tough time finding out.